The Endless Abyss

Kyle Tianshi

The Endless Abyss

Book Series

The Twilight Overlord

The Eternal Flame

The Endless Abyss

The Endless Abyss

ACKNOWLEDGMENTS

This final book of the series is the longest of them all. The greatest challenge was to come up new ideas and plots to keep the story interesting. Thank you, mom, for oftening sharing your life wisdoms and encouraging me to make notes everyday in order to capture the interesting dialogs and activities that happened at school. My supporting sister always cheered and prasied me for my hard efforts and kept me perservering. Both of my grandpas were super proud of me being able to write. I would also like to give my deepest appreciations to all my friends who were eagerly waiting for the ending of this book series. You have motivated me to stay on track of finishing the book.

As an eleven year old, I wish I had more life experiences and personal adventures to include in my story. To challenge myself, I am going to join a two-week boarding camp in Beijing this summer to explore the deep history and culture. My next book will feature the many wonders of China, so stay tuned!

ISBN-13: 978-1721525928
ISBN-10: 1721525920

Printed in the United States of America
First Printing, 2018

For My Grandpas

The Endless Abyss

Chapter 1

Before I begin my story, I want to say an apology.

If you've experienced a few (okay, maybe a little more than few, but what's the difference) cataclysmic or destructive events, I'm sorry. This apology is especially dedicated to those who were near Oceanside Pier, Sequoia National Park, the Smoky Mountains, and other weird places during December.

I know you were trying to enjoy Christmas and stuff (I didn't get any presents from Santa), but this just had to happen.

I hope you have insurance to cover your costs, and again, I'm very sorry.

…

I felt like a total failure.

Oblivion had been released, and I didn't really do anything to stop it. And when he came out of his box, I was absolutely terrified.

He looked like a dark spirit, full of hatred, writhing and thrashing. A movie played on his body, showing terrible scenes so horrid that I'm not going to recount them. But then, he made a choice.

And of course, I couldn't do anything to stop it.

The spirit seemed to survey everyone, and it rushed toward David.

"STOP!" I yelled. Like that would help. But, of course, I was too slow, and David was possessed by Oblivion. I'm not sure if that was good for his health.

When he opened his eyes, they were completely dark, full of horrifying pictures.

And there you have it. We have our newest (and final) enemy, ready to destroy us. And he was one of our friends. Oh well.

"Solaria and Cataclysm, we must leave now," David spoke in Oblivion's voice.

"Why?" Cataclysm whined. "Can we…"

"I said, no!" He waved his hand, and the mansion rumbled. It would only be a few moments until it collapsed.

"C'mon, Mumbo Jumbo," Selena said, gathering me up in her arms.

"Please, brother?" Cataclysm pleaded.

"Can you hear, or are you deaf? Perhaps I should take-" They all disappeared in a puff of black smoke.

Selena flew me down to the ground, and the mansion collapsed in a heap. I looked up at her and said, "Find everyone else. We'll need their help to find Paul."

"Okay." She flew off, and I closed my eyes,

feeling the touch of the rain on my face.

…

Sometime later, Selena arrived back with Yohan, Sarah, Nina, and Hannah. I saw that Hannah's eyes were red, but she just stayed silent. It must have taken a really long time for her to find them because the sun was setting down the horizon.

"Guys?" I said.

"Yeah?"

"Um… can you go off to find Paul first? I sort of… well… I need to talk to Selena."

"Sure thing," Yohan agreed, and he walked off with Sarah back to the ruins of the house. It seemed that Nina and Hannah were friends now because they were talking to each other (or, at least Nina was talking, because Hannah kept her face buried in her hands).

"What is it?" Selena asked. I turned to look at her and said, "I sort of feel like a failure. You know… we thought that we won. But in reality, we really… didn't. I mean… now that pit in New York is expanding."

"The Endless Abyss," She nodded.

"I don't know. Maybe… I should have been possessed by Oblivion, you know. I could try to control him."

"No way. I don't want you to leave my side,

ever, because you're dear to me. I… I think Hannah's handling it well, but I wouldn't stand leaving you. Even if you're annoying sometimes." I blushed and smiled.

"Okay."

"So, promise me that, okay? Don't leave me… ever."

"I promise."

"Thanks."

"Okay. Are you ready to find that Paul guy?"

"Absolutely not."

"Well, then, isn't that great?" She got up, surveying the horrible mess before us.

I pretty much gave up on finding Paul right away. We walked through crumbled stones and wrecked furniture, kicking things aside, but there was no sign of him.

The wreckage of the mansion was heaped up in huge piles, and we didn't know where the entrance for the basement was.

"I give up," I declared after five minutes of pointless searching. I sat down on a pile of rocks and sighed.

"C'mon, Will. We can find him."

"No, we can't!" I stomped the ground, frustrated, and I heard a creak. "Um… I think we found the basement." We dug away the rubble and uncovered a trapdoor.

"Sure we can't," Selena smirked.

"So, do you have any of your famous plans?" I said.

"First thing, though. We need to get everyone else over here."

"Yeah." I flung open the door and peered into the darkness. "Guys! I found the basement!" We crept down the stairs, and I cast a light rune down the darkness.

"Mmm mmpphh!" a muffled voice yelled.

"Paul? Is that you?" The basement seemed pretty bare, and there was no Paul in sight.

"Mmmm mmmppphh mmh!"

"Coming! Where are you?" I turned to Selena. "There's nothing in here. Maybe he's in a wall."

"What?" Nina growled. "How would he be in a wall? Your brain is probably in a wall!" I wanted to protest, but Selena held me back. "He's just giving an idea."

"Mmmmmm!" I turned to where the sound was coming from and walked to a wall. Selena kicked it, and it flew open. Then I realized-it was a door.

"Well… you're smart," she said.

"Thanks, Airhead. Paul! Where are you?"

"Fffmmm-" His voice suddenly stopped.

"Um… there's something else in that room," Selena whispered. I peered into the dark hallway and spotted a door at the end.

"Should we get the others?"

"We should hurry. I think whoever's in there will know that we're here. Then they might leave soon."

"Okay… are you sure?"

"Are you really scared of the dark? C'mon! Whatever's down there can't be that bad, can it?"

She was really wrong.

…

Inside, there was a huge, bright room, with a pile of explosives in the center. The walls were smooth and white, not like the rest of the basement. Then there was Paul strapped to the side of the bombs with a stick of dynamite stuck between his teeth. But the weirdest part was the monster. She was a Selenian but had steampunk goggles and a green hat on, and instead of two flaming scimitars, she held an iron wrench.

"Uh… hi," I mumbled, not sure what to say. "Um…"

"Hello!" she chirped. "What can I do for you today?" She took out a lighter and ignited the fuse for the bomb.

"Um… oh yeah…" Selena flashed a smile. "We… um… we…"

"We… we wanted to check out your explosives! They look really cool. We needed some for her birthday party, right? You know… to blow something up."

"Wow! Finally someone appreciates my work! Everyone was like, use your two swords, but I really don't like fighting. Wrenches are a lot better. What type of bombs do you need?"

"Um… we-"

"Well, let's clear out of here before we make the deal, 'kay? This guy's gonna blow."

"Wait!" I yelled. The fuse was shortened to a stub. "I- we- wait! Put it out! I want to check out those bombs!"

"You do? Okay!" She rubbed her finger on the fuse, and the flame stopped.

"Thanks!" I slowly stepped forward and pretended to examine all the bombs. Selena looked at the spot behind tied up Paul and asked, "What type of bomb is behind Paul?"

"C-4 and dynamite."

"Really?"

"Yes! Of course! Do you not trust me?"

"No. Could you…" She peered over Paul's head. "Could you untie this guy? I… I can't really see anything." She hesitated for a moment but nodded, and untied Paul's bonds.

"See? It is C4. I'm not lying."

"Thanks!" I called, summoning a destroy rune and throwing it at the pile of bombs. "Go!"

"Hey!" she squeaked. "You didn't pay yet! It's going to be ten million dollars-" We sprinted away, but not quick enough. The force of the explosion blew us forward, and I conked my head on a sharp rock.

"Why…" I croaked, but I passed out before I finished my sentence.

…

"He… hello?" I mumbled, opening my eyes.

"He's awake," Yohan announced. He was standing above me, and Selena was crouching right next to me. The sun was rising over the horizon, but chilly blasts of air swept through the land. It wasn't raining anymore.

"Merry Christmas," Selena said, standing up. "I don't think you got any presents today unless someone drops them for us. By the way, I hope you didn't lose any brain cells."

"Oh, shut up," I grumbled.

"Mmm-hmm."

"Is everyone else okay?"

"Pretty much," she answered. "You got a concussion, but it's nothing we can't fix. And we've destroyed half the property. What were you thinking, back there?"

"No idea, Airhead."

"You're the Airhead in that case. Can you get up?" I was a bit dizzy, but I managed to stand up.

"We really should go," Nina muttered, who

apparently didn't care too much about my health (surprising!). "Will Bill, you've wasted a lot of time."

"Will Bill?"

"Yeah, whatever. How will we fly? Can you guys conjure any magical flying creatures? Anyone?"

"Oh," Paul mumbled. "About that… I can sort of summon a phantasmal dragon."

…

A few minutes later, we were soaring above the clouds on a translucent, light blue dragon, flying to Aer's palace to report my failures.

"My mom might give us some information," Selena said, the wind blowing her hair into my face. "You know. Maybe some helpful allies."

"But she hates me. There's nothing we can do about that."

"At least I don't hate you. She might not like you, but she wouldn't harm you with me at your side."

"Thanks… I guess."

"Also, I want to drop Nina, Hannah, and Paul off at Fort Azari. They're… well… I just prefer this group, you know. Fighting Yharon together."

"Yeah. But they might not agree with us, you know."

"Uh huh…" She stared at the fluffy clouds beneath us. "I feel like we're getting close here."

"And where are we again?"

"Alaska."

"How quick does your mom's palace move? I mean, it was hovering above Fort Azari when the god convention happened."

"It depends on the wind," she answered. "And today, the wind's blowing pretty hard, as you can tell."

"There it is!" I exclaimed, pointing the island, hovering two feet above the ocean. "Wait… what? Why's it… falling?"

"Um… I really don't know. Maybe… it'll be fine. Don't worry." She sounded plenty worried.

"Really?" A part of the island dipped into the water. "I don't think so." We swooped down into the fields next to the lake in Aer's palace.

But something was wrong. The grass was blood red. The lake was crimson. All the trees were withered and gray.

"Oh," Selena said quietly.

"Yeah. Everything's okay here."

"What… what happened?" Sarah asked, coming up from behind us. She patted Selena's shoulder. "It'll be okay."

"Mom!" she called. "Mom!" Her voice echoed through the empty palace. The wind blew a bit harder and formed a translucent spirit that transformed into Aer. She had on a flowing white robe, and for some reason, had white hair.

"Selena." She rushed forward and wrapped her mom in a hug.

"Mom… what… what happened? Please… please tell us."

"Why do you have white hair?" I said. By the way, sometimes I ask brilliant questions sometimes.

"Oblivion. When my kingdom is destroyed, I will lose my power. Become a regular person. If you can stop him, I will come back. I heard that he got released, by the way?" She looked up and glared at me.

"It's not his fault, mom."

"The truth is, I'm not sure what happened. Oblivion must have come in and corrupted this place. I was going to check on the other gods, but I'm here right now."

"We… were going to see if we could find any allies. You know. I wanted to ask you."

"Most of the gods and goddesses are in disorder," she answered. "But… there are a few things I can tell you. Abyssion might-"

"What? NO!" I interrupted. Then I realized what I did and lowered my head. "Sorry… we've had… some bad experiences, to say the least."

"He can help against Solaria and Oblivion. He could poison this crimson menace and maybe help. But Selena. I want to ask you to do a favor for me."

"Okay. Definitely."

"I need you to check on all of the kingdoms of the major gods. To see if they are plagued. To give me hope that we can still win. Can you do it?"

"I can," she responded confidently. "But... do you have any other suggestions? I mean, for allies?"

"I've been watching your conversations." We both turned bright red. "And I heard that you needed a mount. Other than your dragon. Do you want another dragon? A fire one, to be specific. Her name is Betsy."

"No way!" Yohan said. "She was fighting against us a few years ago. But we captured her, right?"

"But do you remember where she went after that?"

"Well... no... but-"

"She got captured by the sun monsters again. She's in a cage, somewhere hidden in Yharon's jungle, with a few sun monsters guarding her. And by the way, the sun monsters still aren't on our side."

"That's great," I grumbled. "So we can get two of our enemies as friends? Fat chance."

"Quiet, Will," Selena ordered. The island tilted to one side, and we all lost balance.

"How much time do we have, anyway?"

Nina asked, speaking up for the first time.

"By the looks of this island," Aer judged. "You'll have about one day. Probably until midnight. But who knows about the other kingdoms?"

"Okay then," I said. "First stop, the stupid ocean?" The island groaned and shifted, water seeping through the edges.

"No. First stop, we drop some of you off. I'm not letting all of you go to do this. Only four people. We need to spread out our forces evenly."

"What?" I exclaimed. "But-"

"You heard me. Now go."

...

Well, that delayed us a lot.

I was hoping to drop Nina, Hannah, and Paul back at Fort Azari and take off to wherever. Unfortunately, that didn't happen to well.

As we came close to the borders of camp, I saw a landscape of crimson grass, dead trees, and no living thing in sight. It was at least a mile away, but still was going at a steady pace.

"What has Oblivion done?" I muttered, staring at the ground.

"I don't know. Hope this place lasts longer than... than my mom's palace... you know."

Right after we arrived at Fort Azari, I

13

proposed, "Me, Selena, Yohan, and Sarah can go. You guys can just stay here."

"What?" Nina yelled, hopping off her dragon. "No way. You four have already been on quests together. Why don't we get a chance?"

"Do you really think that you can do better than us?" I demanded. "I don't think so."

"Just because you're a stupid elemental and have one of your dumb legendary weapons doesn't mean that you can just be a jerk head!"

"Well-"

"Why don't we both go off on our own paths, huh?" she said. "We'll see who's better! Right?" She turned back to Hannah and Paul.

"Well," Paul sighed and hopped off the dragon. "I know about Fort Azari, but I've never been here. I spent all my life in China." He looked all around.

"Wait… what? Is there even a cabin for Alluvion?" I asked.

"Um… about that…" Selena lowered her head.

"I really just want to stay here," he decided. "I mean… I've lived my whole life, running away from monsters, but… I mean… this place feels safe. I just sort of want to stay here for a bit."

"Sorry guys," Hannah said. "I want to go with Nina. Also to keep a lookout for David. Just… you know."

"Where do I go?" Paul asked. "Do I stay-"

"Yeah," Selena grumbled. "We… well… we don't actually have… a cabin for Alluvion."

"Oh."

"But isn't Sarah staying in the Aphelion cabin? Because… well… she's sort of related to fire?" I said.

"Yeah, but nothing really relates with all that misty stuff and Alluvion, you know. I mean…"

"Really? Then I could-"

"You can use my cabin," I suggested. "There's a bunk bed, and I only use the bottom one. You can take the top. Sorry if it's not organized or anything."

"Thanks." He smiled at me gratefully. "I guess I'll…"

"Where're your parents, anyway? Won't they notice."

"Oh." His face darkened. "It's none of your… oh well. I guess I should tell you."

"No, it's fine if you don't," Yohan said nervously, fidgeting with his hands.

"I will. I… I had a mom, but she died. I also had a sister, a little sister called Kam. But she disappeared when my mom passed."

"That's sad," Sarah mumbled.

"But my dad… well… I guess I sort of lied. Alluvion is my dad. But he barely pays attention to me. He's too busy with all of his stupid war things."

15

"Don't worry," I promised. "Now, are we going to go, or what? First stop, um… where?"

"Aquaia's place is under Oceanside Pier, but I want to go get a proper mount," Selena said. "Darkecho, here we come."

"We can look for David too," Yohan suggested, gesturing at Sarah. "And also check out the kingdoms. Do you want to meet back at Aer's palace at… I don't know… Eleven-thirty?"

"It's already pretty late right now," I muttered. "What if we can't do it?"

"It's winter, Mumbo Jumbo. The sun sets early. It's only about… six right now. We got plenty of time."

"Good luck everyone," Nina said. Then she turned to us and glared at me. "Except for you."

Chapter 2

I really wish we agreed Darkecho's request of building a house for him in Fort Azari.

Because we now had to fly all the way to his modern house in the Caribbeans. By the time we arrived, the sun had pretty much set.

"Darkecho!" I called. "Hello?" Suddenly, I felt a huge, warm tongue on my back.

Right here, man!

"Eeek!" I squeaked, turning around. "Glad-"

"Eww," Selena said. "Why's… why's his spit… purple?"

"What?" A blast of cold water drenched my face. Darkecho grinned. His wing had splashed me. "No… what was that for?" I spit a glob of seaweed out of my mouth. "You know I don't like water, right? Now... now I need a towel or something."

"Take my jacket," Selena said, unzipping it and throwing it to me. I caught it, surprised that it was so light. I examined the gray surface, seeing if it was made out of any unique material.

"There ain't any cooties on there, just saying."

"I know. Just… thanks anyway." I summoned a flame and warmed myself up a bit, but it didn't help.

Where are we going, man? Shopping at the

mall? I've always wanted a suit! Brownies?

"Sorry," I shivered. "The world is sort of ending, and we need your help."

WHAT? No… no more brownies?

"Gosh, buddy," I grumbled. "You nearly shattered my eardrums there… in my mind… maybe? I don't know. But we need your help to fly. These… these worms we've been using are not good. They're scary to ride on."

Yeah! I'm the best, man!

"Uh huh. Now, could you fly us there?"

"Sure!"

…

I never realized that flying creates lots of air resistance on you, and blah, blah, blah. The point is, in one minute, I was totally dry by the wind.

And then, in five minutes, an ocean came into view.

"There it is!" I exclaimed. But something was wrong. All the water was pulled back.

"Wait a sec," Selena said. "Doesn't… doesn't that mean that there will be a tsunami?"

"But… but a tsunami… like…"

Here it comes! Bye, peeps! Darkecho tilted, and we started falling down and landed on the pier. I spotted a dark wall of water rushing toward us.

"Well, here it comes," she sighed.

"What do we do? I mean… is Aquaia the one doing this, or… or someone else?"

"This might be crazy, but I think we have to fly into it."

"Um… are you sure?" I said. "I really do not think that it's a good idea. Maybe… maybe something else?"

"We don't have time to decide right now, Will! It's coming right at us right now!"

I didn't have anything else to suggest, so I nodded, and we flew straight to it. One second before we entered, I whispered to Selena, "Good luck."

"You too." And we dove into the water. There were a few moments of black, and then images appeared in front of us.

A dark blue fortress loomed in the distance, its walls crumbling. Then it changed to Oblivion (or David, it's way too confusing) tearing through a fiery palace that seemed to be Aphelion's kingdom.

A voice whispered, "Think happy thoughts. That is the key to defeating him."

Finally, we came out of the water (we were dry!) and landed on a hard wall. I took a deep breath, taking in some air.

Wait, air? This definitely wasn't good.

"What… what was that?" I moaned. Selena seemed to be a lot better than me, and she helped me up. I felt dizzy and fell into her arms.

"Are you okay?" she asked.

"Fine…" A brimstone fireball flew over our heads and smashed into something behind us.

"This place might have some problems, though." She waved her hand. "Let's go, Mumbo Jumbo."

We immediately smashed into a huge hulking figure that was firing some weird black projectiles at whatever was outside the fortress.

"Oh… sorry!" I yelled, and we went around it.

"Sorry what?" a familiar voice grumbled. He turned, and I realized that it was Abyssion.

"Um… nothing," I muttered and pulled Selena away.

"What the heck, man?" she said. "That was him. Didn't you notice? Now, what do we do? Go back to him and say, I'm sorry!"

"Well, if he realized that we hit him, he definitely wouldn't help us."

"Well yeah… but…"

"So it's better to be nice. We're in enemy territory, sort of. Better to be careful."

"Um… Abyssion?" I called out.

"Who is it?" He turned around again, and I was surprised at how he looked. Instead of a colossal squid thing with a shell, he looked like a watery man, wearing a blue suit (what's with all the suits?) and tie in his thirties. Weird.

"Sorry," I mumbled. "Wrong person, I guess."

"Do you people not recognize me?" he said. "I am Abyssion! Now, what do you want? You're wasting precious time here!"

"Why do you look different?" I asked, ignoring his question.

"Oh, shut up. Do I look that bad? I hope not. I am the god of the deep sea, and… well… the son of Oblivion. So I grow stronger as the void grows stronger here. And…" Another fireball flew over our heads. He closed his eyes, and it turned into a whale, which fell onto the ground, flopping like… well… a fish out of the water. Then it disappeared into mist. "Why can't they stop on the fireballs? I can't control all of them!"

"Um… yeah… so… we need your help-"

"Why… are you so… nice?" I asked. Another stupid question. "And do you not remember us?"

"Nice? Excuse me?" I was splashed in the face with some brackish water. "I'm just happy that Oblivion's boosting my energy level. And, to answer your second question, why would I remember puny demigods like you? Or maybe I do remember you. You smell." He took a turquoise flask from his pocket and tossed it over the wall.

"Where… where is the enemy?" Selena said.

"Oh… Cataclysm's just lobbing fireballs

from a distance right now, but they're advancing. He's with several hundred Oblivion monsters too."

"Uh huh. So… can this place handle it without you?"

"Definitely not. Why would I leave this place? We need to defend it, right?" He tossed another flask overboard.

"Uh… yeah."

"We gotta protect Aquaia. If her fortress falls, then she will lose her power. Not good. After Oblivion conquers all the gods, he will only have to wait for the void to swallow up the earth god."

"What's his name again?" I asked.

"He doesn't have a name, dummy," Selena grumbled. "But… well…"

"So you puny demigods want me to attack Oblivion? Not a chance. We should let him attack us. But we need to strike down his helpers first. Cataclysm here, and Solaria somewhere else. I think at Aphelion's fortress. Now help me fight this dude or leave to your little demigod parties."

"We-" But one look from Selena's face told me to shut up. "Okay." The walls shook. "What do we do?"

"What do you do? Go out there and fight them! Take this just in case." He stretched out a thin hand and handed me a flask.

"What good would one flask do?" I complained. I was sure that Selena would give me a beating after this situation was over.

"Well, you can't actually consume it. Give it a throw." I wasn't sure but chucked it over the wall. An image of the flask flew out and shattered against the rocky ocean floor. Bolts of blue energy flew out and started tracking the enemy down. When the blasts contacted with a monster, it would explode and disintegrate them.

"Oh… wow," Selena said, and I could tell that she really wanted to use it herself.

"Just go out and fight them! We got reinforcements in the keep, so you'll have backup, okay?" I nodded and asked one more question. "Why is there no water around here?"

"All Oblivion. He knows the water empowers us, so he's taken it from around the castle."

"That's good," I mumbled.

"What was that?"

"Ahh… nothing. Thanks for everything!" I grabbed Selena's hand, and we jumped over the ledge.

…

I never knew that draining Aer's power would remove Selena's power too.

We did not have such a soft landing on the mossy marine rock, and I felt a sharp pain up my left leg. I sat on the ground and winced.

"What happened?" Selena asked, turning around.

"Nothing. Is… is your power been taken away because Aer's power is being taken away too?"

"I don't know. That was a pretty hard landing, though."

"Better not to think about it. By the way, do you want this flask.?It seemed like you wanted it badly."

"I did not!"

"Yes, you did! Well, do you want it or not? Cause-"

"Okay." She held out her hand and wondered if she wanted to help me up or to hand over the flask. I decided to do both, and I felt my leg. It was fine.

"Now remember, dummy," she said. "There is no water here, so you could fall and crack your head open. And there seems to be a ravine ahead of us, which might stop Cataclysm for a bit. But you can fall too."

"Why can't you fall?" I complained. "I find it a lot better that way."

"Because I should be able to fly."

"Should."

"Yeah."

"So you're not one hundred percent sure?"

"Yes. Now, we're wasting time here. Also, a

thought. That tsunami thing up at Oceanside Pier. I think that that's the missing water from down here. Oblivion is trying to cause as much destruction as possible."

"Then how would we stand a chance?" I said, thinking. Then, a thought popped into my mind. "When we were headed down here, a voice whispered in my head. It said: Think happy thoughts, and that's the key or something like that. Maybe…"

"Just maybe."

"But it's our only hope right now, so… I guess we have to do it. Give it a try when we need it. When you're going against Oblivion."

"How about, when we are going against Oblivion," I corrected. "I'm not fighting him by myself."

"Nah. We'll be eating popcorn and watching from the sidelines."

"Okay then. I hope you're ready for this. Hey, Cataclysm!" she yelled, across the gash in the earth to the army that was standing ahead. "Are you too stupid to cross the ravine? Or are you too afraid?"

A fireball exploded next to our feet.

"Um… there isn't any chance of the water putting out the fire, right?" I whispered.

"No. The only way to put out brimstone flames… well… you can't. You just have to let it burn until it dies out."

"There's no way to put it out?" I scratched my head.

"There's no way."

"Well, that sucks."

"It sure does. Do you have a plan?"

"Me?" I said. "I got nothing. You're one with all the plans, right?" The ground exploded with red shrapnel.

"How about surviving this stuff?" she decided, jumping away as another blast of brimstone flames exploded in front of us.

"Great idea! How about some traps?" I suggested. "If you could... like

"Really? In the ravine? I'm sure that won't work."

"Then let's do it."

...

Why is Selena so good at everything?

She managed to set up a whole bunch of rune traps around the ravine while dodging all the blasts of fire that Cataclysm was sending.

Me? Well, I was tripping and falling all over the rough terrain, barely dodging all the fireballs flying past me.

And in the end, I only set up a few traps (one backfired and exploded in my face). Cataclysm's army was marching around the ravine and was halfway through when we finished.

"Ready?" I called.

"Here it goes!" The ground exploded at the edge of Cataclysm's army, and blasts of green water blew out and gave some Oblivion monsters a good shower. Unfortunately for them, the water was toxic, and they disintegrated into a pile of ashes on the spot.

"Nice!" I yelled. But the monsters were a bit warier now, and they discovered some of the traps (Selena claims that those traps were set up by me. I wish I could argue, but I was pretty sure that she was correct).

"Oh no!" she cried. "We are out of traps, RIGHT Will?"

"What? Now we're- Never mind! Yeah! Oh no! We are out of traps!" A monster exploded into toxic fumes, which immediately spread to the other enemies, making them explode.

But now we really were out of traps. Half of the enemy was gone, but few hundred still were there, along with a very mad Cataclysm.

"Retreat?" I said. "We… um… yeah-"

"NO!" Abyssion bellowed from behind us. "Stay there! Just…" There was a loud pop, and a few hundred allies appeared in front of us. They all were mermen like figures, bearing blue-green shields and broadswords. "There you go! All yours!"

"Okay then. Defend?" The front line locked shields and formed a barricade.

"Nice," I muttered. "Ready, Airhead?"

...

Oblivion and Cataclysm use some really cheaty tactics sometimes.

The monsters held up flamethrowers (I want one!) and melted our barricade with brimstone flames before we could do anything. Not fair.

"Can we leave?" I wondered. "Please?"

"Shut up!" Selena answered.

"Does that mean yes or no?" Cataclysm's army advanced, and the army lifted their swords and charged.

Selena chucked her flask all over the place and exploded many monsters, but more just kept coming. I drew Malachite, summoned some of its swords, and started casting runes.

I jumped into battle and slashed down rows and rows of monsters, arrows flying near me but none hitting me.

Finally, I worked my way to Cataclysm, who was busy fighting a bunch of allies. This was the perfect chance. I drew my knife and prepared to bring it down on his armored head.

My blade collided into his helmet, and he

crumpled to the ground. I smacked him again, and he teleported away.

Monsters jumped on top of us, pushing me down.

"HELP!" I yelled, my voice muffled from the enemies on us. A guy with a spear prepared to stab me, but I rolled out of the way and bumped into a fallen warrior.

"Will!" Selena called. "Will! Where... are you? Are- OW! Stupid hammer... You okay?"

"I'm... GAH!" The monster slammed his spear down again, but suddenly went limp and turned into dust.

"Thanks," I managed, spitting some out of my mouth. "We... we need to go... now."

"Too... many?" She raised her arm and blasted a group of monsters with something on her wrist. Then I remembered, two years ago, when Selena and I got Vesuvius from Yharon's seat but were branded for the act.

"We-"

"Duck!" A flaming arrow flew over my head.

"Thanks! Now let's go!" She grabbed my arm and pulled me along. "Everyone, RETREAT!" We climbed back up to the front wall where Abyssion was sitting, drinking a cup of tea.

"Why... why didn't you help?" I complained. "And... you're... you're just... you know."

"No complaints, kid."

"They're… they're… too strong," Selena sighed, rubbing her arm, which had been smashed by a hammer. "Ow… this… this hurts."

"Oh well." He waved his hand over her arm, and she straightened up.

"Thanks. Oh no! What's the time? We still need to check on Aphelion and Cryos and… I don't know what! Before… before my mom…" She lowered her head and closed her eyes.

"She what?" Abyssion said. "Don't leave me on a cliffhanger here!"

"Fades… away…" she mumbled. "If… if only Oblivion could be stopped. We came here to see if Aquaia's fortress could survive any longer. That's why we have to check on everyone else. If all the gods and goddesses fall, it's… it's over."

"Uh huh. I think I got this place covered for at least one more day. But I'm-"

"You're that good?" I muttered.

"-not sure. Could you come back here after you finish your silly quest? I have something down in my lair that might help this place's situation. It's like… well… I'll remember someday."

"What?" Selena groaned. "You would remember… someday? We don't have that time! Meanwhile, there's that pit in New York that's expanding and it's going to consume the whole-"

Abyssion said, "You little demigods know about the Endless Abyss too? Well, I'm guessing that it'll speed up its process of eating the world every time a god or goddess, because every god dying is less good power in the world. But that is just more power for me! Yay! It's about eight right now, and you said that needed to check on Aphelion and Cryos? Easy. Aphelion's located in Mount St. Helens.

"Where's that again?" I said.

"Washington, Mumbo Jumbo."

"So, like in Virginia?"

"No. Washington State."

"If you would take a look at the news…" He waved his hand, and a blue T.V. appeared in front of us. There was a picture showing a smoking black mountain in the distance, exploding over and over. It seemed that the whole volcano was swarming with red ants like it was an anthill, but I realized that they were all monsters.

A tall, fiery figure stood in the center, wielding a massive blade. Another thing was darting around it like a fly, trailing some weird blue dust. I guessed that the big guy was Aphelion and the fly was Solaria (if she had heard that comparison, I'm not sure she would like it).

The weirdest part was the huge, blue storm raging around the mountain. It wasn't raining, but enormous bolts of lightning were flying down and colliding into the rock.

The camera flew closer but suddenly started

making a weird buzzing sound. The screen went black, which still makes me wonder what happened to the camera.

"That there is Aphelion's place. It's a lot stronger than Aer's little baby palace, but if they manage to get in the volcano, we might have problems. And now Cryos's castle is on Mount Evans-"

"You mean Cryos's fortress is that little cabin place that's hanging on the edge of that place?"

"Of course not! Have you been there before?" What is my imagination, or was he growing bigger?

"Well… yeah. Like two years ago." Selena seemed lost in thought.

"Whatever. Cryos's fortress is at the top of the mountain. Oblivion sent his main army to attack that one. Do you want to watch some more T.V.?"

"No," Selena answered. "Please… no. I… I can't." She took a shaky breath. A blast of brimstone flames flew over our heads.

"It's not safe here anymore," Abyssion decided. "Even with my super protection-"

"You've been protecting us the whole time?" I said.

"Why have all the attacks flown over your head? Why have you survived? I hope you know the answer. But I need to stay here. Just remember, be careful."

"What about Galaxius and Reality?" I wondered. "Wouldn't they still be okay because… um…"

"Nah. Reality's already down because Oblivion's breaking him, stretching him to the max. Also, you know, he doesn't like his children because they feed off him. So… about Galaxius. He's still okay, probably will be the last god standing. But his power comes from all the other gods. So once the Earth falls, he falls."

"And Abaddon and Alluvion?"

"Abaddon? How did he get to your side anyway?"

"Well, he said that he would join our side if we got both of the legendary weapons, right? You know… that prophecy."

"That thing? He would agree to that?" the god laughed. "That might work, but I don't think so."

"Is… what?" Selena said quietly. "I… I…" she shivered.

"You okay?" I asked, sitting next to her. "Look. You can tell me what's wrong, okay? Please."

"No… I… I can't. I'll tell you later… It's… nothing." She rested her head on my shoulder.

"Whatever," Abyssion grumbled. "I don't care. You know what the two weapons stand for?"

"No."

"Well, Malachite symbolizes the Earth, and Vesuvius symbolizes the sky. You know. Meteors falling. Sky. You get the connection?"

"Oh." I felt sort of stupid. Luckily, Selena wasn't really herself at the time, so I escaped her wrath.

"But your silly weapons probably won't work. The Earth is getting destroyed, along with the power of Malachite. Same thing with Vesuvius."

"But why doesn't Oblivion just poison all of the kingdoms, just like Aer?" I suddenly asked.

"Obviously, Aer's palace is the weakest of all-"

"Shut up," Selena whispered.

"Well, that's not nice."

"I don't care."

"But it takes power to do that. He wouldn't have near the amount of energy to destroy one more kingdom. Well, I haven't gotten the time for you peeps. Come back at... I don't know when, but soon. I have a task for you to do that might save this place. See you later! Bye bye!"

"I have a question-"

He waved his hand, and we appeared in the middle of the tsunami.

Chapter 3

Luckily, (or unluckily, I don't know much about tsunamis) we ended up on top of a tall building.

"Where… where are we?" Selena mumbled.

"Wake up!" I yelled, shaking her arms. "Tsunami! Bad!"

"What? Oh! Okay! We need to help the people!" The building tilted to one side, and we starting sliding off.

"NO!" I screamed, grabbing at some handhold. Right before I could fall off, a steady hand caught me.

"Hold on!" Selena squeaked. "I… I can't hold you. Just…"

"Let go! I'll be fine!"

"I won't leave you! Just… we'll fall together, okay? We need to find a tall, sturdy building. Then we'll survive. Just-"

"Don't worry! I'll be fine!" I let go of her hand, hoping that she wouldn't be stupid enough to follow me.

I fell, and the wind whipped around me. For one scary moment, I couldn't fly and was just dropping like a rock. Then, I took a few deep breaths and calmed myself down. I started floating, and I went up, looking for my dragon. I looked back at the building I just came from.

Selena was gone. Where could she be? Maybe she went back down the stairs… no. She wouldn't do that.

"Where are you going?" she asked, right next to me.

"Gah! Sorry. You scared me there for a moment. Darkecho. We need to find him now!" I yelled. "DARKECHO!" No answer. Nothing.

"Okay then," she whispered. "Find a building for me, okay?" I scanned the area.

"This ain't New York City, okay? Darkecho!" I thought I saw a dark shape hurtling toward us.

"Can't… hold… on!" We started falling down, but only for a second, because we landed with a thump on a dragon.

Brownies!

"Hey man… Fly to Mount Saint Helens, please."

Brownies for life! Woohoo!

"Thanks. Selena! You okay?"

"Um… ow… I… I think so. Maybe. I'll be fine…" She sighed, and I righted myself up.

"Why were you acting so weird back there?" I asked. "You said you would tell me, right?"

"Yeah. You know how it feels when you lose someone dear to you."

"Oh."

"But I know that I'm going to lose my mom, and I can't do anything to stop it. She might be mean to you, but… you know…"

"I know. I'm sorry."

"It's just like… if you lost your mom." A tear streaked down her cheek.

"Okay," I said, feeling maybe a bit uncomfortable. "I'm really, really sorry. We'll find a way to fix it. I promise."

Yummy brownies! Darkecho yelled from up front.

"Your dragon has some serious problems," Selena sighed. She wiped the tears off her face and turned back to my crazy dragon.

"Hey Darkecho."

Hiya, man!

"Um… are we close to the mountain?"

What mountain? Oh yeah! That mountain. There's that big pile of brownies that's swarming with red ants? Mmm…

"Wait, what? Is that it?"

Mmm hmm. Mount Saint Helens. Great place for vacations and stuff, you know.

"Selena, we're here," I reported. Everything looked the same as I had seen from Abyssion's T.V., except that the fire god was missing from the center of the volcano. "You ready?" The air around us turned hotter and hotter until I was sweating like crazy.

"Hot," she panted.

Hot? Not hot! Brownies! He dove for the mountain.

"No! Darkecho! Stop! Those aren't brownies!"

No brownies? Oh! Yummy fly! He gestured his giant head toward Solaria. I nodded, and he dropped us off, ready to eat the delicious fly (I really hope Solaria doesn't find out about her comparison to a fly).

"Too… too hot…" Selena muttered.

"You… you don't have any ice cube rune?"

"Might have one, but… but I can't do it… can you?" I nodded and imagined a bunch of ice cubes. An avalanche of ice cubes. There was a rumbling sound coming from the volcano. I suddenly felt like I had to throw up, and thousands and thousands of chunks of ice exploded out of the mountain, showering everyone in the radius. But it didn't stop there.

The mountain started belching snow, covering the whole place in the stuff. I'm not sure if Aphelion would appreciate this. Then the clouds above rumbled, and it started hailing large chunks of ice.

"Good enough?" I screamed as a boulder smashed into the ground right next to me.

"A little too much!" she yelped, summoning a protective field around her. "Here, c'mon!" She reached out her hand and pulled me in.

"Thanks," I grumbled. "You happy now? Now let's go back out and-"

"No! Your energy must have been drained there. Stay down for now." Now that I thought about it, I realized that I was exhausted.

"Thanks." Fire streamed over our heads like fireworks, and I wondered what other humans would think about this.

"As long as you don't fall asleep or go into a vision, you'll be fine, okay?" Selena said. "Just-"

Too late.

...

A dark, misty fortress loomed in the distance, surrounded by hills shrouded with a dense fog. I realized that it was probably Alluvion's kingdom.

Two figures watched the palace from the top of a tall hill. I came in closer and saw that it was Oblivion and one of his monsters.

"Really? Why this place first?" the monster grumbled.

"Well, Alluvion is just a minor god but can be very annoying at times. You realize that he is the one who took down Yharon and helped defeat Abaddon. Better not to underestimate him."

"But sir-"

"Excuse me?" He summoned a huge cleaver

from the air and brought it to the monster's chest. "You better not anger me, monster. Otherwise... you know the-"

"Ow!" David yelled as if he was back to his own self. "Stop-"

"Just adjusting to this mortal," Oblivion said, grimacing. "Sorry. GO! Get the elite soldiers ready!" The monster nodded and scurried away.

...

"-don't-"

"Um... hello?" I said.

"What was that? Were you..."

"Captured in a vision," I finished. "Just what you didn't want me to do. But I did it." A chunk of ice smacked into Selena's shield and destroyed it.

"Okay then. Break time's over," she said. "Now let's go." We rushed up the steep mountainside, trying to avoid all the chaos around us.

Finally, after some really close calls, we reached the peak of the mountain, which was still spewing snow. I saw Darkecho flying above us, showering Solaria in purple flames.

"Now how do we get in?" I wondered, peering over the edge. I only saw a boiling pot of lava with frost blowing out of it. The blasts of ice and snow were slowing down and turning back into flames.

"Runes."

"Of course," I grumbled. She summoned a glowing orange rune that she said would give us fire resistance.

"Thanks," I said, and jumped into the volcano. Two seconds later, I hit the lava and bounced right back to the top of the mountain. Selena came flying out too, right after me.

"This… this might be a bit harder than expected," she muttered. "It's like a bouncy house. Just don't break your legs if you get launched out."

"Great idea. But-"

"No time! We're surrounded!"
Unfortunately, she was right, and that we had to go. "C'mon now!" She grabbed my hand and pulled me in.

…

Have you ever wondered what it would be like to have a swim in a nice, bubbling lake of lava?

Well, I have some suggestions.

Don't do it.

It felt like my skin was burning right off my body. I was glad that my clothes didn't melt off the second we hit the pool.

I struggled to swim out of the water, partially because I really didn't like swimming and such.

But we managed to get onto the hot brick walkway, and I noticed an entrance into the depths of the cavern.

"That way!" I said, and we rushed to it. The room inside seemed to be a meeting hall. There were rows and rows of cushioned chairs facing a large platform holding a golden chair, designed with intricate runes. The walls of the place were dark purple, and torches were set on them.

Two monsters were trying to lug the throne away.

"Stop!" Selena yelled. Well, we can't make a sneak attack now.

"Huh? Is that you, your majesty?" One of the monsters turned, and I saw that it was a Selenian.

"Mmm hmm," she growled in a strange voice. I almost burst out laughing, but the Selenian seemed to think that she was Solaria. "You two idiots don't know how to do a thing!"

"Wha… what?" the other monster mumbled. "Did… did we do anything wrong?" I pulled Selena behind a chair and asked her what she was doing.

"Some don't have very good eyesight. Have you been listening in monster class?" she whispered.

"Uh… no. Whatever. Just go with your plan." I was pretty sure that her plan was going to work.

"You two, leave the room! I'll deal with the

throne!"

"But… make sure to destroy it. It is the source of Aphelion's-"

"Do you think that I'm stupid?" she demanded. "I know what I'm doing! Get out, now!"

"Yes… yes your majesty." The monsters bowed and left. They were walking right past us when the Selenian paused and looked at Selena carefully.

"Wait… you aren't Solaria, are you?" She drew a solar sword and pointed it at her throat. Selena suddenly smashed her on the head with Vesuvius, but it barely fazed her. The Selenian slashed the blade across her arm, leaving a huge, burning cut.

"OW!" she yelped and fell into a seat. Coils of rope started rising from the ground, and before I could do anything, we were tied up.

"Well, well, well," a female voice said, her voice echoing through the large room. "Look who we have here. Some surprise guests." I looked up and saw a glowing figure, wearing a cape walk into the room.

"Solaria," I growled. "You stupid… what's… what's that?" She was dragging something from behind her.

Help… please! The fly got me!

"Darkecho?" I felt tears spring to my eyes. "But…"

"Oh I'm sorry," she cackled. "But your dragon is mine now. Aphelion is busy fighting my army outside. You have no hope. I will destroy Aphelion's throne, along with you."

"Fat... fat chance," Selena mumbled. I finally came to my senses and realized that she was still bleeding.

"Sure," she snorted. "Well, it's time to say goodbye to Aphelion."

...

They threw us on the ground next to the throne, and I healed Selena's wound as best as I could.

"Thanks," she managed. "I really hope that... you know. Aphelion comes in and... saves us."

"Mmm-hmm." I wasn't really paying attention to what she was saying.

"So, your vision. What was it?"

"Hmm? What..."

"Will!" she scolded. "Were you paying attention at all?"

"Mmm... no? What did you say again?" She sighed and repeated what she said.

"About that vision. Well, it seemed like Oblivion is going to attack Alluvion's fortress, which is located... where? Do you know?"

"The Smoky Mountains. The place is full of

fog. But it's interesting that he would attack Alluvion. I guess he thinks that he's actually a big threat to his glorious plan."

"You think we should check that place out to see how it's doing? For your mom, you know."

"Nah." She shook her head. "Although he is powerful, he isn't one of the main gods, so we shouldn't. After this, we have to check out Cryos's palace-"

"If we can get out of this."

"C'mon Will! Think positive here! We are going to get out of this place, somehow."

"Sure," I grumbled. "How, exactly?" The cavern trembled, and molten rocks started falling from the ceiling.

"Stop right there!" Aphelion yelled, falling straight through the roof and landing on his throne. "I'm sorry, Solaria, but you were too slow."

"What? You can't defeat me!" She, along with the rest of her army rushed forward, but Aphelion disappeared, along with his golden chair.

"Well, that didn't help too much," I muttered.

"He… he has to do something! I mean…" The room shook again, and another barrage of rocks fell down.

"Is this his plan? Trying to smash Solaria and her army, along with us? I hope not." Boulders started falling down, crushing chairs and monsters. I summoned a shield around us, but it probably wouldn't do any good.

A dark shape loomed over us, and a rock hit my forcefield so hard that I blacked out.

...

"Will? Selena?" a male voice called. "Where are you?" I groaned and opened my eyes. A purple shape covered me up, and I realized that it was a wing. Darkecho's wing. He had saved us, or me at least.

"Here!" I croaked. "We're... here!"

"Where? What's... what're these purple rocks-"

Hey! That's... that's... me! Brownies?

"You're... you're alive?" I gasped.

Of course, man! But your friend... she's... well... um... I can't find her. I don't know where she went.

"What? But..."

I'm sorry. You could look for her if you want, but we're running short on time. It would probably be better-

"NO! Oh... I'm sorry, but we have to find her." Sunlight appeared, and Yohan and Sarah came in, both carrying something.

"Hey Will! We... we found..."

"How'd you get here anyway?" I asked. "Weren't you... oh. Is she fine?" Yohan shrugged.

46

"We don't know. She got hit by a bunch of rocks and stuff, but I don't think she's injured that badly."

"That's good. But… we really should get going. To Mount Evans."

…

A few minutes later, we were soaring toward Denver. Selena was okay, as she only had a minor concussion but wasn't conscious just yet.

And here we are! Darkecho called. *Lots and lots of enemies, all frozen! Good breakfast smoothie for me!*

"Wha… what?" Selena mumbled from next to me.

"Hey! You're awake!"

"Mmm hmm." I helped her up, and she leaned her head on my shoulder. "Still a bit dizzy."

"Okay then. Quick recap: Aphelion crushed a lot of monsters. Darkecho saved us. The end."

"That's great to know. But… where are we heading now?"

"Mount Evans. It's our last stop before we report to Aer. By the way, what's the time right now?" She thought for a moment but shook her head. "Too hard… I can't concentrate."

"That's fine. But do you think you'll be ready to battle?"

"Of course! I could probably beat you up

right now."

"I believe you," I grumbled. "Which sort of sucks."

We're here, boys and girls! This ice lady's seeming to hold this place up pretty well. But... A colossal explosion rang through the air. *Never mind what I just said.*

"Um… sure." A tall, icy castle rose in the distance, surrounded by a high wall. Part of that wall was busted, and hordes of monsters were streaming through and pounding on the front gate.

They aren't frozen anymore! Dang it. And I need a cooldown after that hot volcano place!

"Yohan!" I yelled. "You have a plan or anything?"

"We could leave," he said hopefully.

"Oh, shut up," Sarah laughed, slapping him on the back. "Um… tell your dragon to land in the castle and not eat any of those frozen monsters yet!"

Aww!

"Sorry man, but listen to what she says."

Okay, I guess.

"Thanks, buddy."

But after that, can I eat them? Please?

"Sure, I guess. But just make sure you drop us off at the right place? Please? Because landing-"

YEAH! Woohoo! He swooped down low and roasted a group of Oblivion monsters. *Bye bye! Although I usually like medium-rare, not well done.*

48

"That's great! Now get us to the fortress quick!"

Uh huh. He swooped drowsily sideways and tilted dangerously.

"DARKECHO!" I screamed, pounding his back. "Please!"

Hmm? Oh yeah… sorry. Just… those peeps down there look really good. But I'll drop you off first, hmm? Yeah.

"Focus, man!"

Okay! At last, he flew us up to a balcony next to a few frost warriors and dropped us off.

Bye!

"Stay safe!" I called, but he was already off and destroying monsters and babbling about monster filet mignon.

"And just who do you think you are?" a familiar voice cackled. I turned to the row of soldiers and watched as one lifted up his… no… her mask. It was the ice goddess.

"Uh… hello! We come in peace… I mean… um… in the name of Aer and stuff!" I said frantically. I don't think we earned her trust.

"Mmm hmm. And why would I believe you?"

"We were sent by my mom to check on all the kingdoms," Selena declared. "So we came here to see-"

"We're fine!" The castle shook, and chunks

of ice started falling from the walls above us.

"Really?"

"Are you questioning a goddess, human? Hmm? We have this under control, okay, so leave and tell your stupid air goddess that-"

"That you called my mom stupid? Okay." Man, I wish I had Selena's nerve to talk like that.

"No no no no! But I don't need your help! We're fine! Now go away!" The castle trembled again, and part of the railing of the balcony crumbled off.

"Are you completely sure?" she challenged.

"NO! Well yes! No! Well... um... when I rushed up here from my house, I forgot my staff, which might be a bit useful here, but I left it because I... you know... was doing my hair and stuff. A beehive hairstyle is hard to do, and the internet wasn't working, so the tutorial video was buffering, and-"

"So you want us to get it?"

"Huh? Uh... yeah! For sure. Then you can leave. Now go!" I pulled Selena through the open door and quickly talked to her.

"What's with her? She's acting like a cuckoo."

"Of course," she answered. "They're all like that! Abyssion being nice? No way. Oblivion is somehow making them act weird."

"Okay. That's good for us, then?"

50

"Probably not."

"Perfect!" I grumbled. "Then what are we waiting for? We…" The fortress shook, and an ice chandelier fell from somewhere above us and shattered onto the ground right next to us.

"Yeah. I hope we actually get outta here before we get crushed by… um… things."

"How do we get out there anyway?"

"Your maniac dragon. Duh!"

…

This time, I wasn't too sure that her plan was going to work because my dragon was acting really weird.

Darkecho was going out of control, tearing up rows and rows of enemies. He somehow seemed to be glowing a faint purple, and I wasn't sure if it would be safe to ride him. Then it came to my mind that he was a shadow dragon, and, along with Abaddon and Signus, was getting more and more powerful.

"Darkecho!" I called.

Huh? He turned his giant head.

"Darkecho! Come here NOW!"

Oh? Okay! Coming! He flew toward us after roasting a clump of archers that were trying to shoot him down.

"Thanks!" Selena shouted. She turned to me

and grinned. "I told you my plan would work."

"Oh, be quiet!"

"Nah."

Where to go, captain? Darkecho asked me, snorting. *Hurry! No time to lose here!*

"Okay man! Patience. Could you fly us over to that cabin way, way, way down there?" Chunks of ice and snow started hailing from the sky, just like what I did in Aphelion's volcano.

Sure man! Hop on! He flew us over the invading army and dropped us off right next to Cryos's little house. We were here a few years ago, where she summoned some wolves to eat us.

"Ready?" Selena said. "I hope her house is organized."

It turns out, her house was a complete, absolute mess. As I opened the door, a pile of books toppled on top of me.

"Ouch," I muttered, tossing them aside. When we headed in, I was pretty sure that there would be no way to find that staff.

Towers and towers of books, papers, clothes, snow (what the heck?), and other junk surrounded us.

"Um… you can search for it," I suggested. "I'll… um… stay back for a bit, okay?"

"It's a team effort, Mumbo Jumbo!" She grabbed my arm and pulled me into the house.

"Now what?" I kicked aside a mound of

snow. More junk behind it.

"Okay then. We… well… hmm…" She sat down on a chair to think.

"Selena! We don't have time to think of a genius plan! We… I mean you just have to search for it. C'mon!"

"So you want to search?" she answered.

"Ahh… whatever, okay! Just… gah!" I held my head, surprised that a huge headache was starting.

"You okay?" she asked.

"Um… yeah. I'm fine…" I crashed into a tower of newspapers and fell down. "Dizzy…"

"Okay then. I'll search for it. You can rest for a bit." I nodded and closed my eyes.

Smart move.

I slipped into a vision.

…

I saw the tall towers of Aquaia's fortress in the distance. The outer walls were completely destroyed, and the monsters were pounding on the keep.

Cataclysm was teleporting around, blasting holes into the place and causing chaos. Now I could see that Aquaia was losing power.

The vision changed again.

...

A vast, misty rock rose above the clouds. Underneath, there were rows and rows of tall trees. The whole area was blanketed in a thin layer of snow as if someone had covered it with sugar. At first, I had no idea where it was.

Then, a tiny light bulb went on in my head about something that Zach had once told me about. Sequoia National Park.

From a distant mountain, two figures were standing, just like what I had seen from the Smoky Mountains. As a matter of fact, I was pretty sure that they were the same two people who were watching Alluvion's fortress.

"If we take down this place, the Earth will fall a lot easier," Oblivion said to the monsters. "We need to get to those trees, the General Grant and General Sherman trees. Aquaia is close to falling so Cataclysm can come over."

"Yes, sir." My vision faded away.

...

"Will! Wake up!" Selena was shaking me frantically. "C'mon!"

"Uhh? Wha... what?"

"I found the staff thing! But there are monsters, so we have to go! Get up now, okay?"

"Mmm? I… oh yeah. Okay."

"Will!" She slapped my arm. "Hello? Are you completely awake?"

"Huh? Yeah. Mmm hmm. Had a vision and…" Someone started pounding on the door.

"We need to go!" she said. "Find a backdoor!"

"Um…" She pulled my arm, and we went jumping through loads and loads of weird junk.

Behind us, the door busted open, and Selena pulled me behind a large box.

"Wha-" She clamped her hand over my mouth.

"Where are they?" a deep male voice hissed.

"How would I know-" another monster complained.

"Shut up!"

"What do we do?" I whispered to Selena. She showed me Cryos's scepter. It was about three and a half feet in length and just seemed like an oversized icicle with a large snowflake at the end.

"I'm going to use it," she said. I shook my head, sure that it wasn't going to work.

Two piles of snow right next to us suddenly expanded and exploded.

"Gah!" the first voice yelled. That was all we needed. We ran.

…

Luckily, the back exit was easy to locate, and we headed outside. Somehow, a blizzard was happening when we went out of Cryos's little cabin.

"This way!" Selena said, dragging me one way. We snuck around the soldiers and were just about to reach the destroyed front walls when I heard a monster from the cabin declare, "There's nothing in here! Let's move!"

"Hurry!" I urged.

"I am! Now how do we get back up there?" The storm around us grew stronger.

"Rock climbing?" I suggested. "Up to that mountain next to the castle?"

"You are crazy," she snorted.

"So that's a yes?"

"Um..."

"Did you get my staff?" Cryos's voice screeched from above. "You better, because I do-"

"Of course we got it!" I yelled back. "But how do we get in? Could you like... open the doors or something?"

"No. But this blizzard is preventing the enemy from doing anything for about five minutes. Good luck rock climbing!"

"She's absolutely crazy," I mumbled. "Well, I hope you're good at climbing because I'm not."

...

Luckily, she was good at climbing. Really good.

I almost fell a few (maybe a bit more than a few, okay?) times, and she caught me every time.

Finally, after a few close calls, we made it to the top.

"Now we have to jump?" I complained, panting. "Like… five feet? C'mon! I… I can't…"

"Really? This is the easy part, dummy! It's a two-foot jump! You fall a bit, but..." She sighed, grabbed my hand, and we jumped back onto the castle.

"You made it?" Cryos said, appearing in front of us. "Really?" She started giggling like a crazy maniac for a few seconds.

"Um… are you okay?" I asked, backing up a few steps, nearly falling over the edge.

"Careful, Will!" Selena snorted, catching me.

"I'm… I'm good," Cryos said. "But thanks for the staff. I'll be good for now." She snatched it from Selena. "Bye!" She disappeared in a burst of snow.

"She's real cuckoo. Really, really weird. But we better get back to Aer, huh? Where's Yohan and Sarah?"

"I think they're down there fighting," she answered. "We better get them."

"Okay then. Now, to get back down…"

"Get your dragon, Mumbo Jumbo!"

"Yeah. Okay. DARKECHO!" Five seconds later, he appeared through the snow, carrying Sarah and Yohan.

Hey man! Got your buddies here! It's getting a bit cold, huh? He shook some of the frost off his back, spattering us with it.

"Thanks for the snow. Now, we really need to get outta here soon, okay? Please?"

Aww... C'mon! Can we just stay-

"NO!" I snapped. He bowed his head, ashamed.

"Oh. I'm sorry buddy."

Don't worry about it.

...

After a short ride, we arrived back at Aer's palace, which was not looking so hot. Two sides of the walls were completely broken down, and the whole island was half submerged in the ocean.

"Mom!" Selena called. "Where are you?"

"Selena," Aer said. The wind blew, and a flickering, pale spirit appeared in front of us.

"You're okay!" she exclaimed. "Mom." She tried to hug her, but her hands passed right through her.

"I'm sorry, Selena." She reached out to touch her face, but she couldn't. "How are the kingdoms?"

"Well, Aquaia isn't fine right now, but we're going there soon. Aphelion's okay, but part of his fortress got… well… blown up. Oblivion's planning to attack Alluvion and Cataclysm… I think… he's going to go after Sequoia after he defeats Aquaia."

"Thank you. I… well… thank you. I love you Selena. Stay strong." Her voice faded away, along with her body.

"No." She sank to the ground. Oblivion's voice boomed, "One goddess down. Only a few more to go."

"They're here already… oh," Hannah and Nina walked up from behind us. "Um."

"You two are a bit late," I snapped. "Aer's… um… well… she's gone now. And… um..." I knelt down beside Selena. "Are… are you okay?"

"Mmm hmm," she said. "My mom's gone. We're definitely okay."

"Look. It's not the end of the… well, it is sort of the end of the world, but we can fix this. We just… you know… have to defeat Oblivion. Easy."

"But…" She closed her eyes.

"She's not gone, okay? We can get her back!" A weird sound, like cracking, filled the air.

"But how? It's just…"

"You'll be okay!" I said.

"Sure, then."

"Um… guys?" Yohan interrupted. "The island's breaking up."

"Okay then. Let's go back to Aquaia's fortress for Abyssion."

Chapter 4

Yohan, Sarah, Hannah, and Nina wanted to stay at the surface and help the carnage that happened. And by the way, the place was a complete disaster. The pier was strewn across the beach. Buildings had collapsed onto streets. I was actually glad that I wasn't going to help clean up.

"Hold on a sec," I said to Selena after we landed. "If… um… Aer's gone, for now, aren't your powers gone too?" She shrugged. "Kind of. But I still can help."

"I believe you."

"Thanks." She flashed a smile at me. "Well, we better go now. I hope Abyssion's doing well down there." We waded into the water, and it swallowed us. There was a second of darkness, and we fell right on a wall, next to Abyssion.

"You're back, eh?" he asked. "I hope you'll be quick enough because these peeps have destroyed everything. We're down to this keep now."

"Where's Aquaia, anyway?" I grumbled. "Shouldn't she be helping her own kingdom?"

"She is! She's inside there, in the vault, controlling everything!" He raised his hands, and a barrage of water washed the monsters.

"So, I was once going fishing, and there was

this cute little fish, like the size of a couple Empire State Buildings, all stacked together."

"Wait, what?" I interrupted. "You call that little? That's enormous! But, no stories, okay! Can-"

"Are you being rude?" he asked. "You don't want me getting mad, that's what I'll be telling you."

"Um… never mind. Go on."

"Well, it came out of the ground, and I captured it. But it started shaking and tried to get away. In the end, I stopped it, but he sent a huge wave, like a tsunami. So I took a bottle and captured that too. And I put it down in my base down in the deep sea, and it's still sitting there. I was thinking, we could open that bottle and get the water to flow back in."

"So you bottled a tsunami, and we're supposed to get it," I said.

"Mmm hmm. It's easy! No one can find my base, because it's so hidden!"

"So…" Selena muttered. "We can't find it either, right?"

"Right!"

"How do we find it, then?"

"That's your own problem! Right… um… never mind that. I have to tell you, or you won't find it." He nodded, seeming proud of his logic. "I have some goggles, and if you wear them, you'll find a path to my lair. If they're working correctly, a path of rocks will light up. Good luck!" He brought forth two pairs of goggles that looked exactly like what the Solarian steampunk at the mansion was wearing.

"Um… I've seen those before," I said. "A monster was wearing them."

"Really? Then that might be a problem. Whatever. Bye!" He waved his hand, and we teleported to the outskirts of Aquaia's fortress.

"Well," Selena sighed. "We have no idea what the bottle looks like, or what's down in his base. That's great."

"Oh well. We've done plenty of impossible things together. I only hope that his little hideout isn't as messy as Cryor's house."

"If it is." She started grinning. "You can search for it."

…

Luckily, Abyssion's goggles worked well. When we put them on, a clear path of glowing stones traced its way down the ravine that Cataclysm's army had crossed earlier.

"How do we get down there?" I said. "I'm not rock climbing again, just saying."

"Well, follow the path." She pointed to the glowing stones, and I saw tiny steps, carved into the marine wall, leading down.

"I am not going down there!" She took a look behind her and frowned. "Quick, we're being followed!"

"Okay then. Let's go." The stairs were steep and slippery, but Selena helped, and we managed to make it to the bottom.

The lighted rocks traveled down into a dark cavern, and then deeper down. Then I realized that the nonwater area ended here.

"Um… I don't want to go down there," I said. "There's water, and I'm really sick of using runes."

"Oh, come on. If you're not going down there, I'm still going. You can wait here." I was not going to see her go down there by herself. "Alright. I'll go down there. I know that there's some water breathing rune, and I hope we don't get crushed by pressure, but is there any rune for not getting wet?"

She nodded.

…

After a few minutes of diving down into the darkness, it got tough to see. A dense, black fog filled the air, and I panicked for a bit because I couldn't find Selena.

"Hello?" I called. "Selena? Where are you?" My voice drowned out in the deep water. I could still see the glowing stones clearly, but nothing else. Suddenly, I bumped into something. Whoever, or whatever grabbed onto me.

"Get away!" I yelled.

"Stop it! It's me, Selena!" she answered. I stopped fidgeting. "Sorry. I… I got scared for a bit."

"It's okay. I got scared too. Don't worry. Everything will be fine."

At last, the trail ended. The silhouette of a dark fortress loomed in the distance of the large cavern that we were in.

"I'm… I don't want to go there…" I said. "Maybe… maybe… um…"

"C'mon, Will! You can do it!" I nodded and sighed. "Okay then. Sorry. I'm just afraid at what's gonna be in there."

We ran into a problem right away. We couldn't get the front door open. It was at least twenty feet tall, and the handles were way too high for us to reach, even if we had the strength to open the door.

"Well then. Got any ideas?" she asked me.

"We could find some window or vent and try to climb in," I suggested. "That's my only idea."

"Okay then. Let's go find something."

There was a vent that was close to the ground that we used to get into Abyssion's base. Selena hoisted me up so I could reach the metal grate, and I opened it. Luckily, the inside of the vent was as tall as a regular human, so we could walk normally. After getting lost in there for a long while, we finally found another exit.

The room was so big that I couldn't see to the other side, but I could see a tall workbench with a bottle sitting on top of it.

"There it is!" I exclaimed. "But… what are those?" Three sparks seemed to be dancing around the bottle.

"Um… I don't know. Maybe they're defense mechanisms. Or… sun monsters," she said. "Or perhaps they're doing a dance. You want to join in the fun?"

"They're probably enemies," I answered. "Oh well. What should we do? I mean… if we could even get to the bottle in the first place, it would be too big for us to carry."

"Yeah. Maybe… maybe we could just take those monsters out and deal with the bottle afterward. I'm sure we could do something with runes, right?"

"Of course. Well then, I guess we have to deal with whatever those lights are."

…

Unfortunately, those lights weren't sun monsters. They were worse than sun monsters. Whenever we got close to them, we would get launched back. It was impossible.

The bottle itself was twenty feet tall, and the table was much higher. Using runes (of course), we got up to the top.

"Got any ideas?" I asked Selena after getting thrown back by the lights a couple times.

"Maybe we could freeze all of them with runes," she said. "That…" She suddenly tensed and put a finger to her lips. "I hear somebody." She pulled me behind the jar.

"Who is it?"

"-that tsunami in a bottle!" a high voice said. "Right there! Now we just have to get it. More Selenians waiting outside for us. We better hurry, though, because they were pretty grumpy."

"Uh oh," I whispered. "What do we do?"

"Um… wait for them to get up here. I'll… I'll do some kind of distraction when they do." When they arrived at the table, Selena cast a destruction rune past them. They didn't notice it (maybe because they were busy being blown back by the lights), and it exploded on the wall.

"Gah!" another deeper voice growled. "You blowing things up again, monster?"

"N… no sir."

"Then who was it? Go check around the bottle now."

"Yes… yes sir," she mumbled.

"Hurry up!" I drew Malachite and got ready

to strike. Somehow, the knife didn't feel right in my hand, and it was a weird, murky shade of blue, like swamp water.

"Anyone here?" the monster squeaked, peering around the jar. It was the same mechanic that had trapped Paul.

"Yaaah!" I yelled and smacked the monster in the face with my knife. The case shattered instantly, and she was barely fazed.

"Hey!" she said. "Stop it!" She took out a wrench and threw it at me. I ducked, and it promptly hit me in the chest. I yelled in pain and fell down on the ground.

"What's taking you so-" The other monster's voice abruptly stopped.

"Will!" Selena cried, crouching down near me. "I destroyed the two monsters, but are you okay?"

"Ah... yeah..." My stomach was throbbing with pain. "Just... let me rest... I'll be fine." She nodded and answered, "I'll try to freeze some of these lights then." I nodded and closed my eyes, hoping to get some energy back.

"Got it!" Selena suddenly yelled. I opened my eyes, feeling a bit better. Selena had managed to freeze the lights.

"That's great. But how will you capture it?" I stood up, looking around for anything useful.

"I'll think of something. Something with

runes. I'll be fine. Just…" The lights unfroze and started spinning again.

"What's taking them so long?" a new voice grumbled. I gasped and watched as an army of sun monsters marched in, all wearing the steampunk goggles. Selena suddenly waved her arm, and the whole bottle disappeared, along with the lights. She quickly bent down and lay on the ground.

"Sir, I think they must have already taken it," someone else said. "It's not here."

"Alright," the first one answered. "They must have left a different way. Let's go find them. Go!" I waited a few seconds before getting up. No monsters were in sight.

"Good job!" I whispered. She got up too, looked around and said, "I got the tsunami in the bottle. Now let's leave this creepy place now and give this to Abyssion."

"Yeah… but aren't the sun monsters still waiting outside?"

"We can sneak around them easily."

"Really?"

"At least I hope so." She frowned nervously. "Of course we can! When do my plans ever go wrong?"

"Pretty much all the time, I think."

"That's great. Now let's go, please. We need to get back to Abyssion and help Aquaia."

"Okay." I nodded. "Let's go then." We got

out of the giant table and headed back toward the drain that we came through. As soon as we entered, though, we had no sense of direction. Selena pointed down one passageway. "I'm sure that we came through that way."

"No! We entered from the other side, right?"

"I'm confident-" She suddenly paused. "Wait. I hear somebody."

"-taking them so long? Oh! Open drain. Let's check it out," a low female voice growled.

"This way!" Selena whispered, pulling me down one tunnel.

She tried to choose the way she thought would lead us outside, but of course, it ended up in us meeting up with the monsters.

...

"Who's there?" a gruff voice yelled. Footsteps pounded in the passage. We turned into another tunnel. It was a dead end.

"What do we do now?" I said. "We're stuck here and-" I suddenly stopped talking as two monsters walked by.

"I can turn us invisible if you want."

"Okay. Let's hope that sun monsters can't hear too well then." She cast a rune on us, and we snuck out of the tunnel. We started exploring the long tunnels, trying to find a way out. Finally, we found the grate from which we entered. It was sealed shut with some weird red cement.

"What?" I yelped. "Help!" Like that would help.

"What did they do?" she muttered, prying at the grate with her sword. "You think they expected us to come here?"

"Probably not," I said.

"Got it!" She pulled the grate away, revealing the outside of the fortress. "Now let's leave." We hopped out of the pipe and followed the bright stones back up to Aquaia's fortress.

…

Upstairs was a complete nightmare. Crimson fires were burning everywhere (by the way, the smoke coming from them does not smell good). The monsters were swarming over the keep like ants on a piece of bread.

"Open it!" I urged. "They need saving now!"

"Sure. You ready?" I nodded. She took the top of the bottle. Then I found out that I was not ready for what happened next.

The bottle immediately jumped from Selena's hand and shattered against the ground. Then my mind drifted off to other thoughts. How could a container that can hold a tsunami shatter on the ground? Hmm… I finally realized that I was riding on top of a colossal wave toward Aquaia's castle. In other words, it was terrifying. I let out an unmanly scream (don't judge, alright?), and was submerged into the water.

Luckily, our water resistance and water breathing runes didn't wear off yet, so I was fine.

A few seconds later, we arrived at the remains of the wall of the castle. I swam through the wreckage and tried to get a closer look at the battle. The water had washed many monsters off the battlements, but there still were many remaining. I found Selena who was untangling herself from a pile of nets (who knows where those came from), and we headed into battle. I noticed something weird happening, where the crimson flames on the battlements were growing bigger and bigger. Then I realized- brimstone flames grow bigger in water. Why hadn't I thought of that? (And why is Abyssion so stupid?)

"We got a problem!" I yelled to Selena.

"I can tell!"

"What do we do now?" The fire was swallowing the fortress in crimson flames.

"Defeat Cataclysm and leave!"

"Okay!" We made our way toward him while he was defending against a few mermen. I destroyed a few monsters and struck him on the head.

"Yow!" he screamed and turned around. "It's

you again, huh?" I nodded. He raised his sword and prepared to strike. I jumped to the right, grabbed a monster, and held him in front of me as a meat shield. I closed my eyes and felt that enemy evaporate in my hands. I had survived for one minute! Yay!

I got up again as Cataclysm readied his sword once again. This time, I was not as lucky. The blunt side of the blade caught my stomach and sent me flying.

"Ow!" I said, clutching my throbbing stomach after I landed. I looked up and watched as Selena hit Cataclysm on his head. With a satisfying clunk, he fell down.

The flames everywhere died down for a moment, but that was enough. They all sputtered out. Another moment later, Cataclysm rose again, his red eyes blazing with fury.

"Idiots!" he roared. "You-" He fell down again, revealing Abyssion, grinning like a madman.

"That should do it!" he said. "But... he's gone."

"Right here!" Cataclysm boomed from behind him. Abyssion turned and got ready to attack. "You really think you can defeat me?"

"Yes?" Abyssion responded hopefully.

"Now's the time to leave!" I whispered. "Let's get outta here!" And that's what we did. We arrived at the beach to find a few grumpy looking friends waiting for us. The sun was just peeking out over the horizon, which showed the amount of time that we had been down in the depths.

"What took you so long?" Nina grumbled.

"Why? You had a whole city to clean!" I argued. "And I don't see any progress here either!"

"We never volunteered to clean the place," Hannah clarified. "We headed over to San Diego-"

"By hitchhiking," Yohan muttered. "That was Sarah's dumb idea. The guy we rode with had a weird suit and smelly cologne."

"And in San Diego, we went to a restaurant and ate some good food. And we came back and waited here for a couple hours."

"Wait, what?" Selena said. "You went to San Diego and ate at a restaurant while we were trying not to be eaten by a bunch of crazy monsters? That's just…"

"The food wasn't even that good!"

"No! But we were down there in the water, and you were having a nice time? That's just not fair. By the way, where's Darkecho?"

"He started chasing a bunch of pigeons after we left," Yohan said. "And- oh! He's right there!"

Hey peeps! He called.

"Hello," I answered. "Can you carry us to Yharon's jungle? We're gonna get Betsy."

Betsy? His eyes started to look dreamy. *She's so pretty! What are we going to do? Are we going*

74

to meet her? I always wanted to meet her!

  "Uh, yeah. We're going to meet her."

  Ooooh! I can't wait!

  "That's great."

  Can we go now?

  Selena sighed and shook her head. I sometimes wonder what I did wrong to my dragon.

Chapter 5

"So how, exactly, did Betsy get back into the sun monster's hands?" I asked as we flew away from Oceanside. The others were following close behind us.

"Well," Selena sighed. "It's a pretty bad story. While you and Zach were at school, Sarah and I really wanted a break from working around camp, so we took Betsy out for a ride. We talked for a really long time, and we didn't really realize that we were far, far away from Fort Azari by nightfall. I later figured out that we somehow managed to make it to someplace around Quebec in Canada."

Wow! I never knew that Betsy could fly that slow!

"Well," she answered. "It was because we told her not to fly fast because we were just going to have a little fly around. But Betsy was way too tired to fly back, and she started getting a bit sleepy, so she landed down in a field and decided to stay there for the night."

So you and girl blondie froze and turned into ice cubes for the night? Darkecho said, maybe a bit to hopefully.

"No," she snorted. "On our way down, we saw a town nearby and after Betsy fell asleep, we headed over there. It was freezing, but we made it and slept in a hotel room."

Was there free breakfast there?

"Um... no," Selena muttered. "No free brownies or blondies there either."

Well, that just sucks. Nobody should go to a hotel without breakfast!

"Uh huh," I mumbled. "So what happened next?"

"Well, when we came out to the field, Betsy was gone. We had to pay a boatload of money for a terrible train ride back home, and we were punished. Very unfortunate, really."

"But why did you get punished if it wasn't your fault?" I asked.

"Because... um... well... we went out without permission."

That's expected.

"Oh, be quiet!" she said. "At least I told the story!"

Sorry! I'll forgive you if you give me a few thousand boxes of brownies and also give me the two blondies.

"And why would you need to forgive me? It should be me who's forgiving you!" I snorted and thought about how ridiculous this conversation was.

Okay. I forgive you.

"What!"

Yeah! I forgave you. Are you happy now?

"Of course not." And that was the end of that pointless conversation.

…

Land ho! Darkecho called a few minutes later.

"We've been flying over land for the whole time, Purple Face," Selena grumbled. I guessed that she was still a little salty from the talk with my dragon.

Can I drop brownie off right here, in the air? Darkecho pleaded. *I really don't like her.*

"No!" I answered. "And even if you do, she can fly, but-"

Perfect! So I can just dump her off now!

"Wait! No!" He tilted his body, and I just managed to grab onto Selena's hand before falling to my death.

All better now?

"What I was going to say," I muttered. "Was that she can't really fly anymore, so don't do that."

Oops. Oh well. No big loss if she gets turned into to a pancake if he falls.

"Excuse me?"

You're excused. Anyways, we're flying in Yharon's jungle right now, and I don't know where to land. Also, I don't see any building where Betsy would be kept. Do you know?

"Why would we know?" Selena said. "We

were sleeping while he was stolen away, obviously."

Then what do we do? Scan the whole jungle for traces of some secret hideout?

"Um… guys?" I spoke up. "That's what I've been doing the whole time."

Really? We're just wasting time here while we could be roasting the whole place…" He opened his mouth and blew purple flames, turning a big group of trees into blackened dust and some weird purple goop.

"Show off," Selena grumped.

But I did something. And look! He landed in the clearing. *I found something.* Kicking aside a bunch of dirt and pebbles, he uncovered the corner of some old, ancient stone.

"Cool!" I got off my dragon and bent down. "There's a trapdoor here. Let's go in."

"And luckily your maniac dragon can't come with us."

Who says I can't? Darkecho took a massive bite out of the stone and made a much bigger entrance for us. A long, dark hallway stretched on before us.

"Um… I don't think you can come with us," I said, and headed down the passage.

After a long walk (my feet hurt!), we entered a huge room. There was a cage at the end of it, and there was a sleeping dragon in it. A bunch of scattered chairs lay around, and two sun monsters were sleeping in them.

"Whoa," I whispered. "Should I just sneak in and get her?"

"Wait!" Selena turned around and saw a two guards walking down the hall. "Quick… uh…" She cast an invisibility rune and pulled me behind the wall.

"-gonna try to take her out for a walk today," one man was saying.

"No! She'll eat you alive. She's been really grumpy. Probably wants to go back to her old master, whoever he was." Betsy lifted her head and whimpered. She sniffed the air and looked straight at us. Or at Selena (nobody likes me).

"Wake up, you lazy butts!" the first monster called. "We need to be on guard for anybody who would want to take Betsy."

"I'm sure I saw a purple dragon out there," one of the sleepy monsters said, yawning. "But it's probably just my imagination. There's no one here."

"That's what you say every day!" he answered. "But we never know. There could be some people in here right now!"

"Sure," he yawned. "Whatever. I'm going back to sleep now."

"Stupid," he said. "We're going back outside then." I heard the footsteps recede back into the hallway.

"Should I just go for it?" I asked. Selena nodded yes, and I started to crawl forward. The ground was speckled with pebbles and rocks which cut my fingers, but I ignored the pain and kept going.

Getting to the cage was the easy part. But actually getting the cage open without awakening anyone would be difficult. I could just blast the bars open, but I was fairly sure that the sound would wake the monsters up.

I fiddled with the lock (that was very, very hot) but couldn't find a way to break it.

"What are you doing?" a voice hissed from behind me.

"Who is…" I realized that it was Selena, and she was too annoyed at how clumsy I was at breaking the lock.

"Ugh!" she muttered. "You're so slow at doing this thing. Let me."

"Okay. Thanks for the compliment." A few moments later, the lock snapped, and she opened the door.

"See? Easy." Betsy raised her head again and sniffed cautiously towards us. She whimpered and licked Selena's hand.

"Can she talk?" I said. "I mean, like how Darkecho talks."

"No. She's a lot more good-natured than Darkecho."

"Except she doesn't like me. Got it." In return, I was pelted with some rocks. Perfect.

Suddenly, completely out of nowhere, alarms started blaring and the monsters woke up. But that wasn't the big deal. In fact, as they looked at us, they began to run away.

Pistons moved, and slowly, a steady stream of trickling lava polled down into the bottom of the room.

…

"Now what?" I cried. "We're stuck in this stupid room with a whole bunch of lava wanting to burn us."

"Don't panic," Selena said, who was clearly panicking. "What do we do… what do we do… what do we do…" she mumbled.

"Be quiet!" I hissed. "I hear something."

"What? It's probably Darkecho screaming outside about brownies and blondies."

"No… just listen…" We went all quiet, and sure enough, we could hear someone pounding on the wall next to us.

"Hello?" Nina's voice penetrated through the layers of stone. "Did you manage to get yourself stuck in a room? I see some weird stones here." The heat was really getting into us now.

"Um… yeah," I admitted. "We did. Now can

you get us out?" An explosion rang through the room.

"Maybe! I probably could, but the fact that I don't really you two sort of makes me want to leave you in there. Plus, there's a big battle going on out here."

"Well, you need us to help you fight!" I shouted. "Now get us out!"

"Okay, okay- ahh!" Another explosion, much closer this time. "We better hurry! Oh no… what happened to Yohan… But I need your help, Mr. Elemental. I think that we can break this rock using ice. So if we force some ice into the cracks of the stone, it might break…" And she started talking about a bunch of scientific mumbo jumbo (hey, that's me!). I was really just thinking about how she knew about all that stuff. So we just blasted away at the wall with ice for a few minutes (which really drained my energy) until I heard this cracking sound.

And then what happened, you ask?

The whole roof fell on top of our heads (along with a surprised Nina) and melted away in the slowly rising lava (Nina was not melted).

"Well, at least we got out," I said. "Now let's go please. We'll hop on Betsy." Selena and I mounted her but when Nina when on, she reared, and Nina was thrown out of the room and onto the ground.

"She doesn't like the ice," Selena explained.

"Your dragon gets to talk to you?" I grumbled. "No fair!"

"Sarah and Yohan can also talk to her. And we'll be giving Betsy to them anyway, so we can ride your wonky shadow dragon."

"Well let's get outta here now." Betsy flapped her wings and rose gloriously out of the pit. We might have looked really triumphant, but what I saw in front of me wiped the smile completely off my face.

...

So, there was this time when I stole... I mean took some chocolate from the pantry in the kitchen and took it to my room. And as I unwrapped the wrapper on the candy, two crumbs fell from it and landed on the floor. Sadly, I didn't realize, and when I walked back to the kitchen, I noticed that there were hundreds and hundreds of ants just swarming on it. It was insane.

Afterward, I had to clean up the mess, and my mom was really mad at me and hid the box of chocolates somewhere else (and I still can't find it!).

So I learned a few lessons from that story.

One is to be more careful and more sneaky with stealing chocolate.

Two… anyway, that's not the point. The scene that was in front of me seemed like those ants swarming over a tiny piece of chocolate.

So many sun monsters were swarming around a lone Sarah and a lone Hannah and a lone Zach, where they were fighting for their lives on a hill with some magical frost fire barrier that Sarah and one of the frost people had conjured. And, of course, Yohan. He was sprawled on the ground next to them, with a fiery arrow stuck through his stomach. Nina was kneeling next to him, trying to cure the wound.

"Drop us down from here!" Selena commanded Betsy.

"What? But… but we can't fly anymore and… Aaah!" The dragon tilted, and we slid off and plummeted fifty feet down. It was a pretty soft landing, actually, and Betsy roared and plowed through rows and rows of the enemy.

"You see what happened to Yohan!" she said. "You already used a lot of energy in doing that crack the wall thing, okay?" I nodded and was glad that I didn't have to fight.

"You okay? I asked, kneeling down beside Nina.

"What do you think?" she snapped. "Of course he isn't. Now help me with your super healing powers."

"What happened?" I said.

"He was trying to take down all the archers and the cannons that were shooting us from a distance, but I guess... he got shot."

"Will he be okay?"

"Probably, but not for a while. The wound's smoking. Like... literally smoking. Now you're not helping much here, so go fight!" And just as she said that, there was a sickening crack, and our shield burst, letting in a mob of monsters.

I found a fiery blade lying on the ground next to me and took it with me into the fight.

Although our fighting skills were great, we were no match for the rows of monsters streaming through.

"Retreat!" Hannah called.

"Retreat where?" Selena said. "Back into that room you came from. There's gotta be something else down there!"

"Not a good idea," I grumbled. I cast an invisibility rune onto Nina and Yohan so they were hidden from the monsters and jumped back into the pit. The other defenders were also down in the room.

"We found another doorway here!" Zach announced. "Let's go through it, and hopefully..."

"Where are you?" a voice growled above us.

"Yeah... let's go." I said. Hannah opened the door, and we headed down the dank, dark hallway into the unknown.

The hallway was super long and stretched on for at least a couple hundred feet. Finally, at the end of it, a huge, arched door made out of some kind of weird wood sat.

I slowly opened it, revealing a large, rectangular room with a long, red carpet through the middle. Two stone tables lined the carpet, and large braziers full of blazing flames lined the tables. At the end of the room, a huge throne made out of stone and gold (I'm going to be rich) sat on a raised dais. There were two other passages leading further out in the place.

"Smokes, this place is big," I mumbled. "Wow."

"Let's go down those passages," Zach suggested. I think I know what this is."

"Are you sure?" I questioned. "I don't really know. Are you sure that it's a good idea?"

"It's going to take us to our next destination. We need to head over to Sequoia National Park. It's the place where the center of nature is. And I think that some of the enemy are going to attack there, so we should go there."

"But what about Darkecho and Betsy?"

"I already told them."

"How are you sure that this will lead us to the place?"

"Okay, okay. I'll tell you the whole story," he

sighed. "So these tunnels are called the Endless Tunnels. They lead all around the world and can make long distance travel a lot easier."

"Why didn't we use them before?"

"Because they shut down after Oblivion was put in his box. But I'm hoping that they'll work again… well… as you can see, they use Oblivion's power to work. Since he's not at his fullest state, I think that some parts have openings into the void…"

"Hold it for a moment there. What is the void anyway?"

"Well, it's the Endless Abyss. Pretty much Oblivion's home place. He's way more powerful down there than up here. He'll be pretty much invincible down there!"

"So, we're going into some rickety rundown tunnel that has openings into the Endless Abyss and we're not even sure if it works in the first place?"

"Uh… yeah. We are."

"And how does this thing work, again?" I asked.

"It's probably too complicated for your little brain to comprehend," Selena snorted.

"Hey!" I complained.

"Joking. So, you want to go?"

"I guess I'll go, if it's the only way."

Chapter 6

Okay. I have to admit, that choice I made just then was not a good choice.

The hallways were well-lit and bright. So what was the problem?

The problem was that, just a few feet under my very feet, was endless void. If one of us fell, it was bye-bye to them. And the even scarier part was the fact that the ground sometimes crumbled below our feet. Some portions of the tunnels were completely missing.

I would want to tell you all of my frights and horrors down in the tunnels, but that would take too long. Instead, I've chosen some of the few scariest things.

The first happened almost right away. As we stepped into the stone passage, a gate slammed shut behind us. I turned to see that we were now stuck in the tunnels. No turning back now.

Then, the floor started to crumble away. We had to run for a very long time before the collapsing stopped. I peered down into the void, watching the stones fall.

"I really don't think that this is a good idea…" I murmured. We forged ahead, not sure of what came next.

Suddenly, a thick fog rolled in and enveloped the air. Zach said, "I think we're passing by the Smoky Mountains right now. Alluvion's base. Be care…" His voice was swallowed by the dense fog.

"Hello?" I called out. "Anybody?" No answer. "ANYBODY?"

"Will!" Selena's voice said from somewhere to my left.

"Where are you?"

"On your left… here!" Two arms clasped around my shoulder.

"AHH!" I screamed. "Get off me!" I fell onto the ground and tried to twist the hands off.

"Will, stop!" Selena said. "It's just me." I nodded and stood back up again. "Sorry. Let's get out of here." I linked arms with her and hoped never to get lost in the place again.

"What about the others?" I asked. "Will we just leave them behind?"

"Their goal is to get to Sequoia National Park. We'll meet them there." We kept walking forward for a bit, and the fog cleared away.

After that, it was just a matter of avoiding some weak areas in the ground, swinging from some metal monkey bars (that was not fun), and running from a flooded area (I hope we didn't cause that).

We finally came out into a large, flat courtyard. There were tall trees everywhere, and in the middle of them all was the biggest of all, towering to at least five hundred feet. That was also an impressive sight, but what was even cooler was the amount of Grovites rushing around, all carrying weapons and wearing armor. They were all peering over an outlook area, and we joined them.

It was hard to see because lots of mist and fog blotted out vision from below us, but on the ground, many many meters below us, were thousands and thousands of crimson soldiers, all prepared for battle. My confidence of us winning was already pretty low, but now it was at rock bottom.

And leading them was Oblivion.

...

"What?" I exclaimed. "I thought that Oblivion was going to attack Alluvion's place."

"Who knows. Everything is messed up right now. Dreams don't seem to be working at all right now."

"And Malachite's probably going to break completely after this invasion," I muttered.

"Will! Selena!" a low voice called. "How'd you get here?" We turned to see Connor, clothed with bark armor, walking to us. He had a crown of leaves around his head, and I guessed that symbolized that he was a commander of some sort.

"Hello," Selena said. "Are you people here to guard the Earth? I mean, it makes sense that Oblivion would use his strongest forces on the best-guarded place."

"This place is well-guarded?" I questioned. It seemed not too well guarded, if people were defending with wooden swords.

"Yes, it is," Connor answered. "We're located on a high position, which gives us an advantage. And don't underestimate the weapons these Grovites have, they're powerful."

"Okay then." My confidence was not boosted. "Did Zach and Nina and the other people arrive?"

"I didn't see them anywhere… But they must be here, right? Come. I need you to come up to our viewing place."

…

We took a few buses to get to a place called Moro Rock. When I saw the sign that said that we had to hike to get to the peak, I groaned. "Really? We've already walked about ten miles today, I don't think I can go any farther."

"Oh, c'mon!" Selena laughed. "You can do it! I hope you don't need a wheelchair." She grabbed my arm and started pulling me to the path.

"Alright," I sighed. We hiked for ten

thousand miles (at least it felt like ten thousand miles), and we finally reached the peak. By then, I knew that I wouldn't hike all the way back down, so (spoilers!) a cannonball decided to shoot me down the other way.

But that doesn't happen for a while. Connor was talking about how the monsters were surrounding the mountains and were trying to siege the place.

"In case of emergency, we have to evacuate down to the Crystal Cave. But if you could help defend here, it would be really nice," he finished. I nodded yes in agreement.

"But we can't stay here for long," Selena said. "We still have a lot of things to check out… watch out!"

I turned to see a brimstone fireball flying straight at me. It exploded against the rock right in front of me, and I slid down the rock, falling into air.

…

I fell for only a few moments before I smacked into a large purple body.

Hey, man! Darkecho cried. *Are you okay? I saw you fall there! Because I saved your life, do I get brownies?*

"Yes and… no," I responded. "Thanks

though."

Hey! That's mean! He landed back down a the base of the rock, so I guess I didn't have to climb down it. We waited until Selena and Connor climbed back down, and some other guard arrived at Connor's side.

"Sir," he reported. "The outer wall has been breached. Prepare your forces for an attack."

"Oh, please no," I grumbled. "I don't even have a proper weapon."

"Oh, yes," Connor said. "I heard that Malachite hasn't been working too well, but it should have more power since we're closer to the source of its power. By the way, we discovered some more of that malachite you made way back when you just arrived at base. So we made some weapons out of it, and they work really good. Who knows what they do?"

"That's good," I noted. "So, where is this Crystal Cave, again?"

"It's right in front of us, guarding the most powerful tree that powers the Earth."

"And how does that system work again?" I felt a bit stupid not knowing anything.

"There are multiple huge trees around the park that normal humans can't see that power the Earth. If they manage to destroy all of them, we lose."

"Can't they just climb right up this mountain

right here?" I asked. "Or throw fireballs?"

"I'm sure they've thought about that," Selena snorted. "Let's go help out! We're wasting time here!"

...

Next up: more hiking!

We walked along the dirt path for a few more miles (my legs...) until we came to a steep, windy climb up a grassy hill. I heard shouts and yells coming from the top.

"Over to the right there." Connor pointed to his right, where the opening to a cave stood. "The Crystal Cave is over there, and that's the place where we'll all evacuate in case of an emergency. And I hope that doesn't happen."

"Yeah," I agreed.

"Now let's continue up this path." And we hiked for a few more (even more?) miles up the hill, stopping to rest every few minutes until we finally arrived at the top.

Zach, the rest of our group, Darkecho, and Betsy were fighting for their lives with the rest of the soldiers far down below on the twisting path and on a long bridge. Further down, more Oblivion monsters were marching up the hill. Hidden archers were shooting from behind branches and trees, and there were blasts of green magic flying through the sky.

A few hundred Oblivion monsters stood on the narrow path and were trying to fire back at the Grovites, but they weren't used to fighting on the bumpy terrain. We jumped in to help, and the monsters were made quick work of.

The Grovites filed into the path and started taking ground, preparing for the next round of enemies. I started walking forward too so that we could get closer to the battle. Zach, who was standing on the bridge saw me and waved me over to him.

"Hey, man!" he exclaimed. "We got separated for a bit there, but we're back all right."

"Yeah. What happened just then? I didn't see the whole thing happen." He shrugged. "Nothing much happened. We arrived here and saw that Oblivion was sending his troops up here, so we came down to help. Luckily, this terrain really isn't fit for them, so they're having a hard time. Also-"

"Look out!" Selena shouted. I looked up and watched as a brimstone fireball was flying straight at us, fired with the intent of cutting the bridge in two.

But we couldn't move. There were too many people packed in from both sides. The front just started to move, and we avoided the blast. Finally, we got off the crumbling bridge, and I made the mistake of looking down. Instead of the regular ground, it was all blanketed with a thick void, with tentacles reaching out and grabbing on to the rock.

"What the… What's happened down there?"

"Cataclysm's here too," Zach responded. "They know that it's our most well-defended place, so they're just using all their forces here." I looked back up again and saw stormy clouds on the horizon.

"And it's going to… rain soon?"

"The sky's been acting all weird now since Aer's down. We've gotten a flash thunderstorm along with a whole lot of sun in just five minutes. But this storm looks like it's gonna last a while." A strong wind started blowing in, and I heard a cracking sound from behind us. The whole bridge trembled and crumbled into a pile of rubble. Some of the stones bounced down and fell into the void.

"Oh, well… There goes the bridge," I said. "Let's get a move on and ignore that, please." As we walked on, I slowed down and walked with the pace of Selena.

"Hey, Will," she said. "What do you need?" I wanted to tell her that I was really tired and didn't want to fight, but I didn't think she would accept that.

"We're wasting our time here! They can handle the battle by themselves right now. This isn't our battle. We need to move to some other place and do stuff."

"No. That's not right. They need us right now. We're staying here until those monsters are driven down the mountain."

"All right then," I grumbled. "Just saying."

"Mm-hmm." Just then, the heavens opened up, and it started pouring rain. And this wasn't any normal rain. The raindrops were like the size of basketballs, and they were quickly turning the dirt on the ground into mud.

The monsters down below launched another fireball, but this time the water that touched it turned into some kind of red acid that burned away the ground.

"Holy smokes," I said to myself. "We really shouldn't be out here, huh?"

"Oh, c'mon, Will!" Selena exclaimed. "We're just gonna be out here for a bit. Stay strong." She punched my arm playfully.

"Ouch."

"Mmm-hmm. The sun's setting already! So that marks the end of the twenty-sixth of December. Great. I feel like we're running out of time, even when we don't really have any time limit."

"Well, here we are." We arrived at the front line of the Grovites battling. I quickly weaved my way through the mass of people and arrived at the front. The enemy was still far away, and I guess after their first defeat, they didn't want to get close to us. Barrages of crimson arrows were flying over our heads and going over the place, but none hitting us. Selena, from behind me handed me a wooden bow wrapped with greenery and a few poison-tipped arrows.

"Help shoot them down," she suggested. "We'll make more quick work of them." I nodded and started shooting.

We were doing great and almost cleared away all of the monsters when a blood-red bolt shot from the sky and sizzled down right at our feet. The ground exploded beneath us, and I got sprawled near the edge of the cliff. I unfortunately almost got knocked off the cliff, but I managed to stay on.

The dust cleared away and settled down, and in the clearing was a ring of charred, red rock. And in the center of the rock was a bad sight. There was Oblivion (or David, whatever you want to say). He looked just like regular, except he was wearing a pitch black cloak and a pinstripe suit, which was not David's style. Other than that, his eyes were completely black like the void and he was surrounded with a bunch of red spirits that were spinning rapidly, just like the ones around Abyssion's tsunami in a bottle.

"David," I said. Nobody else said anything.

"Not David, or whoever," he answered. "He's trapped inside of this body. And he's not getting out unless I let him to."

"He will get out."

"So," Oblivion growled and took a step toward me. I wanted to stand up and get off the ground, but I didn't think that it was a bright idea. "You're the one who defeated Yharon." The people all cleared a wide berth around him and me.

"Yeah..." My response sounded more like a question than an answer.

"Not very impressive, hmm?" He took a few more steps closer. The whizzing spirits flew right next to my face. I backed up more. I was completely soaked from the rain. Behind me, chunks of rock crumbled and fell into the abyss.

"Get away!" I threatened. "I… um… have amazing powers and stuff."

"Sure," he snorted. "Cataclysm will deal with you." He kicked me, and I fell off the mountain, straight to a bunch of grasping tentacles, waiting for me.

…

Falling? Not fun. But I have a lot of practice, so it was no problem for me. But it's seriously not fun when you know that you're going to be grabbed out of the air with a humongous octopus arm.

Right as Cataclysm grabbed me, I started flailing around for Malachite, which I probably should have seized before he got me (I make mistakes, okay?).

At last, I got hold of my knife and started to slash at the tentacle that was holding me. Now the problem I had wasn't that I couldn't damage the tentacle, it was that where the tentacle would drop me after I destroyed it.

Just as it swung above the ledge overhanging the void, I drove my knife point right into the tentacle. The arm burst into a bunch of purple goop, and I fell to the ground.

I crawled away from the void and pushed up against the rock. Red projectiles were flying out of the pit, and I didn't want to get hit by them.

Hey buddy, Cataclysm's voice said in my head. *Doing well today?*

"Shut up," I growled. "Get out of my head."

Tempting, but no. I'm supposed to capture you, so could you please come back?

"Tempting, but no," I responded, mocking him.

Oh, you don't want to get on my bad side, mister. Now come down! He ordered.

Darkecho? I thought, thinking I might be able to connect with him. *Where are you?*

That purple dragon? Cataclysm said in my head. *I saw him fly away with two people that had blond hair. Probably Aphelists, so they can't handle the rain. Anyways, you're taking too long, so I'm gonna have to take you with force.* I drew my bow and readied an arrow. Hopefully all my archery classes would pay off now.

One tentacle whipped out. I shot an arrow. It was aimed pretty well, but its tentacle shot a red beam and destroyed it.

"Oh, what?" I complained. "Your tentacles can shoot lasers too?"

Yeah? Why not? Cataclysm swung the arm at me and knocked me over. More rocks crumbled from the land I was on. I slashed at the tendril, and it exploded into more slime.

Even if you hold me off for long enough, the rocks will all disintegrate. So you're doomed away.

"That's great. I'll… um… find a way out anyway."

Sure. Now, be a good boy and come out here. Another tentacle came flying out at me. I barely warded off this one and got onto my feet.

"Why don't you show yourself?" I demanded. "You fight me instead of your stupid tentacles!"

Nah. I need to keep the void going around here, and if I turn into human form, the void disappears.

"And that's why you have to talk to me through your head, right?"

Yeah. This time, two tentacles flew out at me, and they all fired red beams. I managed to avoid them, but just barely. I shot another arrow at one arm, and it disintegrated. The other came flying at me, and I felled it with Malachite.

You know that I have an unlimited amount of tentacles. I could just use all of them on you, and you would be dead.

"Uh… yeah." I tried not to think about that fate for me.

You're taking too long! He said angrily. *I guess I'll release all my things on you now.* Suddenly, a dark shape swooped through the cold air.

"Darkecho!" I screamed. "Help!" Ten arms came out of Cataclysm's pit. I held Malachite at the ready, but one knocked it out of my hands. It clattered to the floor, three feet from me.

I got knocked down by one and then got picked up by another. Desperately, I gave one last call: "HELP!" Luckily, help was most definitely on the way.

The tentacle that held me exploded into a bunch of slime and fell onto a large purple body.

Hey there, man! A slightly friendlier voice said in my head. *Doin' okay?*

"Um… no. I left Malachite down there. Would you mind going back down there?"

Sure! Except those tentacles scare me.

"Quick! It's going to fall into the void soon!" He nodded his head (at least it seemed like he nodded his head) and dove downward. Quickly, I reached out and grabbed Malachite, but not before an arm could smack Darkecho. He wobbled dangerously but kept upright.

Get back here! Cataclysm hissed. A sucking noise came from the pit, and we started to get pulled in.

The sucking just kept on going and going, until we were almost within the tentacle's reach.

"Stop!" I shouted. "Just stop!" I took my bow out and shot at the void. It was of no use. Soon, the deadly arms were whacked Darkecho. He blew purple fire back, but it just seemed to char them.

Then I saw the real thing I should have been going for. There, hidden under the mass of flailing tentacles was a big, writhing, red spirit that twisted and turned. Crimson light shot out of it and seemed to destroy rock and power the arms.

Suddenly, the spirit turned bright red and shot a powerful pulsing beam at us. It whizzed past us, and I could feel its power. Aiming my bow, I knew that I only had a few shots at this. I only had five arrows.

I released a first shot that was completely offline. We were even closer to the void now, so close that I could clearly see the spirit. There were blood red faces in there, making terrible noises. I had a feeling that they were Cataclysm's latest victims.

I took a second shot, now that I had a better view. It was just about to hit the spirit, but a laser shot out and destroyed it.

I took out a third arrow and shot it immediately. It sailed through the jungle of tentacles and went smack right on the spirit.

The sucking stopped for just a moment, just enough time for Darkecho to fly away.

Stop! No! Get back! Hey!

He lashed out a tentacle but missed.

"Not today!" I called, and we flew back away from the void. I hoped never to go back there again.

Chapter 7

Well, it turned out that upstairs wasn't any better. Oblivion had done lots of destruction to the pathway, as well as set the forest on fire, but he was gone to somewhere else. I landed down next to where Zach was tending for a wounded soldier. The rain subsided and the clouds cleared, leaving a clear sky.

"Hey Zach!" He turned around, and his face lit up. "You're safe! We were so worried about what happened to you. What did happen to you, though?"

"Well, I fell down, and Cataclysm tried to get me. I escaped, and that's pretty much it. By the way, do you have any more arrows?"

"Yes I do. I'll get them for you later. And our story… well, he just came here for a moment and ravaged the whole place. He's so powerful, Will. I really don't know if we're going to beat him. I don't know if we can."

"Think happy thoughts."

"Okay, then." He sighed. "If you say so. But he just destroyed our whole setup in just a few seconds. And some people… Selena… she got some burns. You should check her out." I nodded and went away. All around me, people were tending wounds and doing things. The area was a mess, and deep in my mind, I thought, *If these fighters couldn't do anything against Oblivion, what could I do? I wasn't any better than them.* I spotted Selena propped up against a boulder. She nodded at me, and I walked next to her and sat next to her.

"The enemy is withdrawing for the night," she said. "So we're free to leave now, if we want."

"Did you get hurt?" I looked at her bandaged-up arm. It was a pretty stupid question. Of course she got hurt.

"Yeah. Oblivion did this thing where he made all the air around him black, like void. And then he made the air explode, and I was in the explosion. The effect… well…"

"Here's a pack of arrows and a quiver!" Zach called. He tossed a green leather sack to me.

"Thanks."

"We better rest up. We also need to decide where to go after this. I wanted to go to Alluvion's place in the Smoky Mountains, but I really don't know now. If this place gets conquered, we're dead meat."

"Let's think about it tomorrow. My brain is already about to explode." She nodded in agreement and leaned her head against my shoulder. Around us, people were laying down blankets, and somebody had lit a huge bonfire.

"Good night, Mumbo Jumbo."

"Same to you, Airhead."

...

In my dream, I was down at the enemy camp, which nestled in a valley in the mountain. I floated toward a big white tent with a crimson flag fluttering on top of it. Inside, Oblivion was talking. "-unleash the cannon already! One quick victory, and we're gone!"

"But... but brother! It's not completely ready yet! It might backfire, or something else might happen!"

"I don't care!" he roared. It sounded like he pounded the table with his fist. "Go! Prepare it now!"

"Yes, brother. It will be ready in a few hours." Suddenly, my vision jolted, and I woke.

...

I eased myself up from my position on the ground. Looking up, I saw that the moon was about halfway from its course around the night sky. I looked back down and looked at Selena. Should I wake her? No. She needed rest. Her arm was hurt. I could do this myself.

All I knew was that Oblivion and Cataclysm were going to do something with firing a cannon, and we were going to lose.

On my way down, I listened to the chirping of the crickets and the distant sound of trickling water. Everything around me seemed so peaceful and tranquil compared to what had happened hours before.

"Where are you going?" Selena asked. I nearly jumped ten feet and turned around. "Goodness!" I said. "Please stop sneaking around like that!"

"So where are you going?" I started walking, and she went up and walked right next to me.

"I got this dream. It was where Oblivion was talking about firing something at the mountain to destroy it. So I wanted to stop it. Hey! Why don't you ever have dreams?"

"Um… I don't," she answered, a bit uncertainly.

"You're lying."

"Okay. I admit it. I have had dreams, and some were pretty bad. But I really don't want to talk about it."

"I know that I may sound a bit curious, but what are your dreams about?" I asked. "I mean, there could be important secrets hidden within the dreams."

"It's not- I'm sorry. It's just that my dreams aren't that pleasant."

"Like what?"

"I'm having dreams about your mom and my dad living in your mom's apartment in Los Angeles. They're fine and all, but I once saw my dad watching the news. It showed a picture of New York. Apparently for them, a huge sinkhole appeared in the center of the city and started tearing things up.

"Mmm-hmm. Is the hole expanding?"

"No. But only because Cataclysm was gone. And in another dream, the government declared the ground safe, and that we could go back to living on it."

"Well that's not a good idea."

"But that's not the bad part. My dad... he wants to return to New York again. And if Cataclysm goes back to that sinkhole and starts to chew away at the earth again, well..."

"Oh. I see. So I guess it's decided. We can go on a slight detour to my mom and tell him not to go back, and then go to the Smoky Mountains."

"Right now?" she exclaimed.

"Not right now, Airhead!" I snorted. "After we stop this whatever that Oblivion's planning."

"Um, why don't we just call down Darkecho for a ride?"

"Isn't this a stealth mission? And he went chasing some rabbits anyway. He won't be back for a while. But don't you enjoy this peacefulness? We spend most our life fighting in chaos, and we don't get time to enjoy nature, and things like this."

"Yeah. You're right. Fort Azari has a peaceful forest, but it's nothing compared to this" she agreed.

It was quiet. But ahead, the brimstone flames of the enemy camp were burning. I peered over the ledge that we were walking. I traced the winding pat all the way down to the enemy camp.

Rising through the center of the camp was a tower, made out of black smoking stone and studded with red crystals. At the top, there was a weird cannon looking thing that was inscribed with a whole bunch of runes. In fact, they were floating off the cannon and flying around, leaving a red blur behind them.

Holy smokes…" Selena whispered.

"I guess that's what we're looking for," I muttered, now wishing that I didn't come down here. "It looks like a death machine."

"Sure does. Now I don't think we can make it down this stupid mountain before- how much time do we have anyway?"

"Cataclysm said that it would be ready in a few hours."

"Well, do you think we can make it down the mountain in less than a few hours? Cause I don't."

"I don't either," I agreed. "We could… maybe take a shortcut down."

"Yeah. I would want to jump down this cliff

too, but I'm not sure how well my powers are working. Or yours."

"True. But we're really really running out of time. I think we have to do it." It surprised me that I was the one saying this.

"Okay, then." She looked over the ledge, and I came up next to her. Down below, there were trees and bushes. But so far away. I wasn't sure if we could make it. I said a silent prayer to gods. *Please let us live. Don't make us turn into pancakes on the bottom of the earth.* Let's hope they heard me.

I leaped off the cliff and fell like a rock.

"AAAAHHHHHHH!" was the strangled noise that came out of my mouth as I came plummeting to my death.

The ground came closer and closer, and I was sure that I was going to turn into a Will patty. Then, just as I reached the ground, a soft wind blew through, and I landed quietly on the ground. The same happened to Selena, and we were down.

"Well…" I said with a shaky breath. "That was scary."

"It sure was. But at least we're down now." And again, we started to hike down the hill to the camp.

At last, we arrived at the outskirts, where sentries were stationed all around the base. Inside, monsters were hustling around, getting the cannon ready for action.

"Now what?" I asked. "Do we… sneak in? And how do we disable it anyway?"

"I'm… I'm not sure." That boosted my confidence a lot. "I'll think of a plan, soon."

"What about runes?"

"I knew you would talk about that sooner or later. Something's happened. I tried using runes, and it doesn't work. I'll find out later."

"Okay. Do you have a plan now?"

"Uh, yeah. A very risky one. We need to be super careful with what we do. We need to sneak into the camp and climb the tower. Then, we use both legendary weapons and stab the cannon. Let's hope it gets-" She was interrupted by me.

"Wait, what? How is that going to work?"

"I told you," she snapped. "It's going to be a really risky plan. Now be quiet and listen! I hope that the cannon gets destroyed, and we'll find some way to escape."

"It's probably going to fail, so let's do it." She nodded, and we slowly advanced forward. We found a hole in the guards surrounding the base and snuck in. There was a straight path all the way to the tower, but voices suddenly came from our left. Selena slipped into a tent, and I followed.

"-heard somebody," a voice muttered to himself. Footsteps sounded past the tent that we were in, which luckily didn't have anyone in it. I looked around the room that we were in.

A whole wall was covered with a large assortment of flaming spears, swords, bows, and arrows. On another, a row of helmets, chestplates, leggings, and boots hung. There was another doorway that led to what seemed to be even more weapons and armor. On a few tables, there were cool bottles filled with bubbling liquids.

"It's an armory," I murmured. "Cool. Can I take some of the potions? There might help, or-"

"No!" she said with a lot of force. "If a potion has a positive effect on a monster, it has a negative effect on a human. So don't!"

"Okay, okay." I peered out into the walkway. "All clear. We can go now."

"Great." We slipped out into the open and crept to the next tent. In this one, I heard voices, and we moved on.

At last, we were at the central courtyard where the cannon was placed. I pulled Selena into an alley, and we listened to Oblivion, who was somewhere out there in the courtyard, who was talking out loud.

"Listen up, you fools!" he hollered. "We're going to ready the cannon now! So hurry up now. I want a quick victory here, and we're off to the Smoky Mountains!" I made eye contact with Selena. The Smoky Mountains. That's where we were headed next.

Again, I poked my head around the corner to

see what they were doing. Cataclysm was standing by, but not in his regular form. He looked like a giant purple portal with tendrils lashing out of him. And all the tendrils were traveling toward the cannon on the tower.

At first, I thought that the void was powering the cannon like ammunition, but that didn't really make sense to my brain. Then I realized. Cataclysm was feeding his power to be fired at the mountain. It was like firing chunks of Cataclysm (the thought of that just sounds weird) at us. It would dissolve the mountain and destroy it.

"Um… sir?" A skinny monster clad in red armor walked up to Oblivion and bowed before him.

"What is it, soldier?" he growled.

"After this finishes, are we actually supposed to go into Cataclysm and appear on the parts of him that are stuck to the mountain?"

"Do you not trust my planning, soldier?" he roared, his teeth clenched. "I sure hope you do. Now get out of my sight right now!" I turned my back to the courtyard and looked back at Selena.

"Gosh," she grumbled. "He sure is grumpy today. Maybe because-"

"Selena! They're planning to fire parts of Cataclysm, basically void, onto the mountain. The void's going to eat away at the mountain, and then the monsters can teleport from Cataclysm into the mountain. And then, well, you know what happens."

"Stop!" I turned and saw the skinny soldier pointing a spear at us. We turned to run the other way. Two soldiers blocked that way too.

"Intruders!" he wailed.

"Quick!" Selena said. "We need to go up! They don't have any bows, so we can climb."

"But your arm-"

"My hand isn't burnt, Mumbo Jumbo! Let's go!" All three of the soldiers charged forward, but by then, we were already onto the top of the tent.

"Wait!" I yelled. "If these are tents, then shouldn't they be a bit unstable? Really unstable?"

"I think that they have to be charmed with magic of some sort. We saw a wall hold up a row of armor. Jump!" We leap-frogged onto the next building. The tower was just ahead, but the ground was swarming with soldiers.

"We're on top of Oblivion's tent!" I suddenly remembered my dream that I had. They'll be more careful around this." Some monsters were already trying to climb up. I knocked a row down with Malachite and then summoned an army of green swords to keep them busy.

I heard a creaking sound. The tent wobbled slightly. It tilted to one side, and I slipped down.

"The monsters are weighing the tent down too much!" I said. "They need to get-" CRACK!

The whole tent collapsed into a heap of tent fabric, monsters, and many other random things. I landed on a glowing orange potion that hummed and throbbed, and I decided to be super smart, so I chucked it in the air and dashed away.

I could only hope that Selena was gone already because the air around the potion exploded into a raging inferno. Looking around, I spotted Selena fending off a few soldiers with her staff. I drew my bow and shot one with my arrow, and I rushed over.

"Let's go destroy it!" I called. "C'mon!" Behind us, the flames were catching on to nearby tents. We started to climb the tower. It was difficult, with the flaming arrows flying past us, but we made it to the top.

"Ready?" Selena looked at me. I nodded and suggested, "What about our brands? We can use them." The fire grew even bigger.

"Okay." We raised our wrists to the sky. The flames died down and started streaming to the marks. I felt the air grow hotter and hotter around us. Everyone down below stopped in awed silence for a moment as they watched the power being taken to our wrists.

"What are you doing?" Oblivion screamed. "Attack!" He raised his hands and started a brimstone hailstorm. Red fireballs rained down from all over the place and exploded onto the ground. Monsters were climbing the tower now, but I couldn't stop and attack. The only thing defending us right now was my green sword army, and there weren't many of them left either.

All the fire was gathered up now in the palms of our hands, and we released it.

Now, we survived all of what happened just then because of Abaddon. Right after we fired the blast, and instantly jumped off the mound and pulled Selena with me. While we were falling, I spotted a shadow ball also flying at the tower. There was a huge roaring sound, and I blacked out.

...

When I woke, we were in the exact same position as we were when we were sleeping, except with a dark hooded figure sitting right in front of us. This time, Abaddon still had his horns, but he wore a dark purple suit and tie instead of his usual armor.

"Um… hey," I stuttered. My head still hurt, and I felt like I had gone through a toaster.

"Hello, demigod. I expected a bit of a warmer greeting to the person who saved your lives."

"Okay, then. Thanks for saving our lives and stuff. Now what happened there? I saw a shadow ball flying down from the air right before I passed out. Was that you?"

"Oh yes it was. So, I was staying at Alluvion's keep, because I was waiting for an attack, but turns out, he never was going to come here anyway!"

"He was going to go to Alluvion's castle right after he destroyed this place," I added. "He said that while we were hiding."

"Well, now he isn't. But Anyway, Alluvion discovered that he was going to use that cannon, so I decided to come down for a visit. I better hurry back, though, because it's almost sunrise, and because Solaria's heading down to the Smoky Mountains."

"But won't you be vulnerable at Alluvion's castle in the sunlight?" I asked.

"Nah." He shrugged. "The clouds and fog there are way too thick there, so no sunlight is coming through. Hopefully, Solaria will be weakened because of that. And I'm getting stronger because evil powers are getting stronger."

"But you won't go over to the bad side, right?" I think I might have sounded too worried there.

"Do you think I will?" The sun peeked its head over the peak of a mountain, and Abaddon winced. "I better leave soon."

"Wait a second!" I called. "Where are all the other gods? I mean, are they helping the battle?"

"Oh. Worried about us poor immortals.

Galaxius is gone missing, all spread out. Reality is completely broken. Everyone else is just waiting in their castles. Signus is having a grand time playing poker in Las Vegas." I wasn't sure if he was being truthful on that one. "And I and Signus can move around freely because we don't have a base to destroy. Because someone already did the honors for us." He glared at me.

"Sorry," I said, not feeling very sorry that I destroyed his creepy, dark kingdom.

"Well, I'm leaving. See you later!" He waved his hand, and he disappeared in a puff of purple smoke.

A few moments later, Selena opened her eyes and shook her head. "What... what happened?" I caught her up on everything she needed to know, and we went to wake up Zach and the others.

Soon, we were ready to leave the mountain to somewhere else. Around us, everybody was getting prepared for battle.

"Now, where do we go?" I wondered. Darkecho flew down from the sky and landed down next to us.

Hey, peoples! Got any brownies?

"No, Darkecho," Zach answered. "We're thinking about where we're supposed to go next."

Well, I would definitely visit Alluvion's base. Learn all the hallways and stuff. I just flew there this night, and it is really confusing. I mean...

really!

"Okay then," Yohan agreed. "We should quickly go there-"

"Oh!" Selena cried. "I completely forgot! We really need to visit my dad. It's urgent. Will and I will go there first, and we'll meet you guys there."

"Okay, then," Sarah responded. "Good luck."

. . .

A few moments later, we arrived at my mom's apartment. I spotted her dad coming out of the front entrance and loading his luggage into a taxi.

"Down here!" I told Darkecho. "Quick!"

"DAD!" Selena called. As frightened as she was, she sounded really excited to get back with her family again. He looked up and made a funny face. We landed, and she rushed up to him and gave him a big hug.

"Oh, sweetheart! What are you doing here? And... is that a dragon?" My mom, who was watching from a distance ran up to me and also gave me a big hug.

"What is it?" she said to me. "Did you need to tell us anything?"

"I'm sorry that we can only stay for a bit," I said. "But Selena's dad really can't go back to New York."

"But honey. The government says that it's safe. We were thinking about asking you, but we decided against it. You're too busy fighting monsters and things. But I'm so glad that you're back!" She ruffled my hair. "But if you really don't advise him to leave, it's fine with me."

"Thanks so much, mom. You're the best." I gave her one last hug, and we turned to leave. I took a look at the taxi driver. His mouth was hanging wide, wide open.

...

We were back in action and flying to the Smoky Mountains in no time. Soon, tall, rugged peaks of mountains were rising from the dark, gray fog below us. In the distance, a silver fortress loomed, surrounded by raging fires. From what I could tell, there was a tall front wall and beyond it was a massive keep. Two towers stood on the front of the wall, and Alluvion and Abaddon were standing on them, wielding some staffs.

We decided to land down next to Hannah, who was getting swarmed by a bunch of fiery guys on the front wall. We fended off the monsters and greeted Hannah.

"Thanks," she said, out of breath.

"Where'd everyone else go?" I asked. She shrugged. "This castle here is impossible to navigate. There's like a billion twists and turns, and I think that the rest of the group got lost in there."

"Okay then. Let's hope that the monsters also get mixed up." We stayed there for the next thirty minutes or so, shooting arrow after arrow onto the enemy. It seemed like some of the Grovites from the encampment were here to aid the battle, and I was glad that they were here. Soon, it seemed like we had reduced Solaria's army to almost nothing when a fresh group of warriors burst out of the mist. Leading them was a grotesque giant, at least twenty feet tall, with huge, bulging biceps and flaming hair. He held an enormous wooden club and was wearing armor made out of some red metal, which basically made our arrows worthless.

This new round of warriors made the other attackers fight harder, and soon we were losing the battle. The giant reached into his pocket and brought out a small orange ball.

"NO!" Alluvion raised his hand and shot a silver beam right at the giant. But he was too slow, and the grenade flew right at the front gate. It exploded, bringing down a huge chunk of the front wall. Shortly after, the blast hit him, and he turned into ashes.

The whole army shifted forward and started streaming into the courtyard. I spotted Solaria darting forward and blasting through the gate to the keep.

"Follow her!" I hissed. We fought through a horde of monsters and finally entered the castle.

Now the only way we could follow Solaria was because she was leaving a trail of sparks behind her. Otherwise, she would have been long gone. But soon, we lost her, but sounds of fighting were echoing from a hallway.

"Here!" Selena yelled. We ran through the passage and found ourselves back at the front entrance. The monsters were slowly making their way into the front of the keep. Another fire giant looked at me and started stormed straight toward me.

"Will you be fine?" Selena asked.

"I'll be good. Don't worry." I managed a smile and turned face to face with the monster.

The giant swung his club at me, and I dove aside. He came back in for a second hit, and this time I tried to deflect the club with my sword. I cleaved the bat right in half, but the force knocked me back into a wall. Roaring, he chucked his splintered weapon at me. There was no way that I could dodge it, but a blast of wind pushed me aside.

"Thanks, Selena!" I yelled.

"No problem, Mumbo Jumbo!" Taking a deep breath, I charged the monster and jumped onto his armor.

"Hrmm!" he grunted. I stuck Malachite through a chink in his armor, and he melted into a puddle of lava. Then, I headed over to help Hannah, who was getting overwhelmed by a mob of Selenians. My mind went into went to other thoughts while I slashed and dodged through row after row of monsters.

But of course I wasn't paying attention, and an arrow grazed my shoulder. Instantly, I dropped Malachite and fell on the stone floor, my arm throbbing with pain. A red flash bolted past me, and my trusty knife was gone.

"Hey!" I said. "Get back here!" The monster who had stolen my dagger was yet another Selenian, and she was flying down a corridor. I sprinted after her and leaped on top of her. She fell down, and I quickly grabbed Malachite.

"Hey!" she squeaked, but I stabbed her, turning her into dust. The next few minutes were spent hacking through monsters, but we were getting overwhelmed. The army had pushed their way well into the confusing corridors of Alluvion's castle.

Solaria was back in action and was creating shields of fire everywhere, blocking off any escape exits.

"Will!" Selena cried. She ran next to me. "We're trapped. Solaria blocked off all the exits." I closed my eyes, concentrated, and boom! The shields cracked and broke into pieces.

"Stupid!" the fire princess snarled. "Your

fighting is useless! Surrender to us now, and we'll make you a commander!"

"No! We'll never side with you!"

"I know that you'll lose. You are hopelessly outnumbered. We will treat you well if you surrender."

"Fat chance!" I said. The army kept on pushing down the hallway, slowly but surely, and Alluvion called, "Form ranks!" A barricade of wooden shields formed, brislting with deadly spears.

"Push them out!" Alluvion commanded. Our forces started marching forward, and we gained some territory.

"No!" Solaria said. "Stand your ground!" She pointed her index finger at the shield wall, and a searing blast of red magic flew at it, blasting it apart. The monsters surged forward again, trampling over the front lines and storming through the hallway.

"What are they doing?" I whispered to Selena. "Don't they need to destroy the whole fortress?"

"No. They're trying to get to Alluvion's throne, which is somewhere hidden in this horrid place."

"Okay, then. Back to battle." We kept battling, formed ranks and pushing the monsters back. But then Solaria would command her forces to keep fighting, and they would always push us back more than we would push them forward.

"We need a different way of doing this!" I said to Selena. "If we keep going about like this, they'll reach the throne room in no time! And we're losing people!"

"You think I'm not thinking of a plan?" she answered.

"Well, no, but still. We need a plan quick. By the way, where are the others?"

"I just went to Hannah and asked. Nina and Zach headed back to Fort Azari because some army of monsters were assaulting it. Everyone else, is here, fighting the battle."

"Oh." My heart sank. Even more monsters were going to Fort Azari? I started to rethink what Solaria had said.

It's useless fighting, part of my mind thought. *The fight is hopeless. We should just turn to Oblivion's side.*

"Shut up!" I growled to myself.

"What?"

"Oh, nothing. Sorry. Just thinking about something." Suddenly, the monster army lines exploded. A purple figure stood in the hallway, roaring. Darkecho had come to save the day.

Get outta here, ugly fire people! He yelled. Opening his mouth, he grabbed hold of a surprised Solaria and flung her into a wall. The enemy was thrown into a panic.

"Yes!" I cheered. The Grovites yelled a fierce war cry, and pushed the monsters back, right into the purple body of my dragon.

"No!" Solaria screamed. "Stop! No! What? Get back into formation!" But the warriors were in too much fright to do anything. Darkecho spewed purple fire everywhere. It was beautiful.

"Fine!" she muttered. "If my army can't do this, I'll just have to do it myself!" She picked herself off the ground and disappeared through a hallway.

"Selena! Hannah!" I waved my hand. "Solaria is trying to destroy the throne! Let's go!" They nodded, and we followed after the trail of fire that Solaria was leaving behind her.

After a long run through many passageways, we reached the throne room. Unfortunately, Solaria was already there.

When I looked inside the room, I gasped. It was absolutely enormous. We could probably fit the entirely of Times Square in the room. It, unlike the rest of the fortress, was made out of a lighter shade of rock and had a long, pale carpet running across it. At the end of the carpet was a raised dais on which the throne sat. It was made of gray and purple smoke and I didn't think that anyone could sit on it.

Solaria was standing before the throne, cackling, "Finally. I don't need that stupid army. I will defeat Alluvion myself!" She raised her hands and prepared to blast it when I picked a stone and threw it at her.

"Stop!" I squeaked.

"You idiots! You think you can defeat me?" Behind me, Selena and Hannah got into their fighting stances.

"Um… yeah? Maybe?" I said. I raised Malachite, and the battle began.

Immediately, Solaria started with volley after volley of fireballs, which all missed. We advanced, and I shot a blast of water at her.

"You can't hurt me!" she roared, knocking the magic aside. "You know- ahh!" A gust of wind knocked her over.

"We can't hurt you?" Selena asked. "Not so much." She advanced, holding Vesuvius in her hand.

Solaria jumped into action, launching fire magic and occasionally summoning disorienting fire shields. I conjured a few of Malachite's projectiles, which glowed a dim shade of blue, like the color of briny water. Probably not a good sign. Selena blasted tornado after tornado, spinning Solaria in circles, and frost was flying all over the room, courtesy of Hannah.

I charged Solaria with Malachite, and she brought out a nasty double-edged axe. She intercepted my swing with it, and Malachite flew out of my hands.

"Haha!" she cackled. "Take-" She was knocked away by a burst of wind into one of Hannah's ice bursts.

"Seems like you're in trouble!" I laughed, quickly scooping up Malachite.

"No! You stupid demigods!" She raised her axe again and swung it at me. I ducked and quickly took a stab at a chink in her armor.

It did absolutely nothing and only hurt my arm.

"Looks like your legendary weapons aren't working so well now," she said. "Looks like Earth and Aer are basically dead. In fact, Aer is dead. Now we only have Aphelion, Aquaia, and these minor gods left. Galaxius is falling, because he's losing elements, and Reality is being stretched to the max. What hope do you have left? Just give up."

"NO!" Selena screamed. I turned. Tears glistened in her eyes at the mention of her mother. "We'll never surrender!" She raised her staff and stormed Solaria with meteors.

"I gave you your chance," Solaria sniffed. "It was a good opportunity. Yet you didn't take it. So now, I'll finish you." She slammed the butt of her weapon into my stomach, and I went flying across the room. Then she picked up Selena with her hand and tossed her aside into a wall. My friend crumpled and groaned.

"Stop!" I said weakly. "Don't- don't hurt her. Please."

"Again, I gave you a chance, but you didn't take it. You'll have to say goodbye to your precious little friend." Raising her hand, she shot a concentrated beam of fire so hot that it burned my hair from a distance. There was no way that I could block it.

Suddenly, Hannah leaped in front of the beam and raised her sword. The spell bounced off the blade and ricocheted right back to Solaria, who wasn't paying any attention.

The blast hit the fire goddess right in her chest. She was thrown backward and blasted into nothingness. Solaria was defeated. Just as she was gone, Yohan and Sarah rushed into the throne room.

"What-" Sarah started, but she stopped. I looked up. When Hannah blocked the blast, a piece of her sword had snapped off and lodged itself into her stomach. She stood there, gasping, and then crumpled to the ground.

"No!" I yelled, quickly getting up and rushing to her. Hannah looked terrible. Her face was pale, and she was barely breathing. Yohan and Sarah were surrounding her too, and somehow Selena managed to get herself next to her.

"Please say that you'll live," Sarah whispered. "Please say that you'll live." But I knew in her heart that she couldn't be healed. Hannah managed a weak smile. "Promise… promise me that you'll be okay. I don't want any more friends getting hurt. Please." She started coughing badly.

"I-" Sarah's voice cracked. Tears welled up in her eyes. "We'll be safe. Don't worry."

I couldn't stand watching anymore. I was also about ready to cry, but I forced my feelings down. Turning away, I stormed out of the throne room.

Chapter 8

I wanted to get away from the throne room. I wanted to get as far away as possible. Thoughts swarmed in my head. My mind told me to cry, but I didn't. After walking for a long while, I heard footsteps behind me.

"Will!"

"Who is it?" I growled.

"It's me, Selena." She grabbed onto my arm. I wrenched her hand away and stuffed my hands deep into my pockets. I said, "Go away. I don't want to talk right now."

"Will, c'mon."

"I said, go away!" I yelled. She put her hand on my shoulder and said, "Really. I want to talk with you."

"Okay," I mumbled, turning around. "I'm sorry. But…" I couldn't hold it any longer. All my feelings came out, and I just started sobbing like a little kid.

"Look. It'll be okay," she comforted. "Calm down. You'll be fine. Don't worry." I know it was weird, but I put my head in Selena's shirt and took a few deep breaths.

"Sorry," I muttered.

"Don't worry." She patted my shoulder.

"I was just thinking. If maybe Solaria hadn't

knocked me down. I could have blocked the shot instead of Hannah."

"Oh, no." She looked me in the eye. "Hannah was one of my best friends. But you've been with me for even longer. We've been on so many adventures together. You've done so many stupid things-"

"You mean, we've done so many stupid things?"

"Sure. We've done so many stupid things together. We're like a family now. Please don't say things like that now."

"Okay. I will." She held out her hands, and I hugged her.

"Will! Selena!" Sarah called. "Where- oh." I quickly released Selena, my face turning red.

"Yeah?" Selena acted pretty cool.

"We need to go back to Sequoia. Connor just sent an emergency signal here."

"What happened to the rest of the monsters here?" I asked. "Did you defeat them?"

"Yes, we did. But we lost many people." She sighed and shook her head. "I still can't believe that we lost Hannah." I really hoped she didn't talk about our friend anymore because I felt like I was going to burst into another round of tears.

"Let's get over to Sequoia National Park," Selena said. "It sounds like they have a battle going on there."

...

We headed out of the Smoky Mountains into great sunshine. It was about noon, and I was already sweating like a wooly mammoth.

"Whew!" I exclaimed, wiping sweat from my brow. "It sure is hot today." Selena, sitting ahead of me, nodded.

Hey, man! Darkecho said. *You got any brownies? Cause I'm hungry.*

"Sorry, man," I said. "We're busy right now. I'll get you brownies after this is done, okay?"

Okay. Hey! We're arriving! Sequoia National Park came into view, and it did not look too good.

The monster army had made its way up the winding path to the peak of a mountain, where the path dipped back down and headed toward Crystal Cave and the giant tree. The Grovites had formed a wall of bark shields and bristling spears at the front, and others were casting spells over their heads and onto the enemy.

"Attack from behind!" Selena hissed. "Drop us here, Darkecho!" My dragon tilted, and we landed in some underbrush next to the main road. Darkecho swooped down, tearing through monsters and tossing them into the air.

"Let's go," I whispered, putting a hand on my tome of spells. She flashed me a smile and nodded. Slowly, we crawled out of our hiding spot and burst out into the road.

I sliced through multiple monsters at once, sometimes releasing bursts of elemental energy. Drawing my spellbook, I spoke spell after spell. Shadow bolts flew out, deadly sleet rained down, and blasts of fire demolished the front row of monsters.

Behind me, Selena was going to work with Vesuvius, whacking soldiers on their skulls and summoning barrages of meteors.

A cheer rose from the warriors fighting against the monsters, and the monsters were forced back down the mountain.

Then, the two Reality Breakers that we trained last summer flew from the sky on a phantasmal dragon with two other people I didn't recognize. Following them was Sarah and Yohan.

Blasts of turquoise magic and mist filled the air, and the monster army was thrown into chaos.

"We're actually doing this!" I exclaimed.

"Quiet!" Selena snapped as she cut through a monster. "Don't jinx it for us! I mean-"

"And WHAT do we have here?" Oblivion's voice echoed through the hills. "FIGHT!"

"Oh no," I moaned. "I jinxed it."

Oblivion was wearing some red brimstone armor and was wielding some kind of scepter. With a chill, I realized that it was the exact same replica of David's staff. He raised it into the air, and the spotless sky grew dark with crimson clouds.

"Hide!" Selena squeaked. Flaming brimstone balls started to rain from the sky and impacted into the ground, leaving behind blazing flames.

One monster who looked like an elite soldier glared at me and charged me with his two flaming katanas. I just managed to bring up Malachite to ward off his swing at me. With a quick strike, Malachite knocked one of his weapons out of his hand.

"Gah!" he growled. "Die, puny human!" He lashed out with his foot and kicked me square in the chest. I went sprawling back and landed hard in a pit caused by a fireball.

The warrior advanced on me and prepared to strike, but a demigod flashed by and destroyed him.

"Thanks," I managed. The person looked at me. She looked like a very fierce Chinese Selena, with brown hair (is a Chinese with brown hair even possible?). But her eyes were light gray and kind of misty, like fog.

"Who are you?" she said, narrowing her eyes.

"Uh… just a fellow fighter, fighting for the good guys. Who are you, anyway?"

"Did you not see me come down on that dragon with my friend and those twins?"

"Well, I saw you. But-" She was gone. *What an odd person,* I thought, watching her tear through monsters with a Swiss Army knife.

"Will!" Selena ran next to me. Her face was all scratched up with cuts and bruises, but she looked fine otherwise. "You okay?"

"I'm good," I answered, then winced as a brimstone ball smashed down very close to Darkecho.

"Then get up!" She held out her hand and hoisted me up. I smiled back at her and got back into the fighting.

"RETREAT!" Connor hollered. His voice was like a deep foghorn.

"Why?" I complained. "We're doing-" Selena clamped her hand on my arm and dragged me back. "Will! We've lost a bunch of people, and we're all spread out! We need to regroup."

"Fine," I mumbled. "I'll go back." Oblivion roared and fired a blast of blood red magic at our newly reformed wall.

The bolt exploded into fiery shrapnel, effectively shredding our defenses and slashing through armor.

"Forward!" Oblivion commanded. His army forged toward us.

"Fire!" Connor yelled. A row of piercing spears whistled through the air and smote the front row of monsters, along with blasts of green magic. I closed my eyes and summoned up roots from the ground to tangle the monsters.

And so it went. There was no apparent winner of the battle; we kept forcing them back while they pushed back. But we were losing fighters, while the monsters seemed to be endless. Every time we defeated one, another would take its place.

"It's time to end this battle!" I said. "Nobody's winning. C'mon! The final push." The sun was setting, and another thunderstorm rolled in.

"I know! But how do we do it?" Selena's eyes flitted back and forth between me and the approaching monsters.

Oblivion himself decided to take a move, and he charged forward, down the path to Crystal Cave.

"Back!" I shouted, firing blast after blast of magic. He slammed the butt of his rod into my chest, and I went flying. Kicking people aside, he charged straight down the hill. We couldn't do anything.

"STOP!" Connor dropped from the sky and landed on top of him.

"Get off!" he roared, raising his weapon. Connor drew a bow and launched five arrows at once at him. One stuck in a chink in his armor, but it was more like a mosquito bite than an actual wound.

Oblivion slammed his staff into the ground, causing tremors to go everywhere. Cracks formed in the Earth's surface.

I got back to my feet and drew Malachite. But I was too worn out to go any longer.

Oblivion drew a sword from the air and slashed down, right down Connor's arm. He howled with pain and dropped his sword.

"You don't stand a chance!" Oblivion screamed. "None of you stand a chance!"

"NO!" Connor knelt on the ground and cupped his ears.

"Oh no you don't!" Oblivion sliced at Connor's back, ripping his armor to shreds. The Grovite started to glow green. Leaves formed around him, and the light kept getting bigger and bigger.

BOOM!

Connor exploded. A boulder fell down my head, and I passed out.

…

"Okay, okay," Alluvion said. I couldn't really see anything since everything around me was just mist and fog. "Don't panic here, elemental. I just wanted to talk to you for a bit. Is that okay?"

"I-" My voice squeaked. "Sure."

"So, you're totally fine. That Grovite saved the day, blasted Oblivion all the way to Hawaii-"

"You're kidding."

"Nah. Would I be kidding? He splashed

down so hard that he created another tsunami. The army will be back at their camp for a while. But just while we're here, I wanted to tell you that Abyssion needs more help. He needs you as soon as possible."

"Details, please?"

"He'll tell you about that later."

"What about Connor?" I asked.

"Oh, you'll have to find that out by yourself. See you later. By the way, thanks for saving my fortress. I hope that girl was worth it."

"Shut up!" I cried, feeling tears come to my eyes.

"Now, now, that's not how you talk to a god like me. But I'll send you back to your world."

...

My eyes fluttered open. My head hurt pretty bad, but I was fine otherwise. I got up, and my heart sank. Connor was lying on the ground, barely breathing, surrounded by my friends.

"No!" I cried and sank to my knees. "You'll be fine, right?" Connor shook his head and managed a smile with his cracked lips. "That... that spell that I did. It uses your life force. I'm sorry. It was the best I could do."

"Why?" Selena moaned. "Connor, please. Not again. Please."

141

"What do you mean… again?"

"Oh," Yohan said. "Hannah. She defeated Solaria. Then… you know." Connor nodded and closed his eyes for the last time.

"No," I mumbled, holding my head in my hands. "Oh no. Sorry. No." I got up and limped away.

Even though I was tired and worn out from battle, I had to take a little walk around.

Again, Selena was after me. He put her hand on my shoulder again, just like last time.

"Will. Get some sleep. You're going to be needing it for tomorrow." I nodded and sighed. I answered, "Sorry. You're right. I'll go to sleep now." Walking out to a spot next to a tree, I sat down and closed my eyes. Soon, sleep took me.

…

The next morning, I woke up extremely early in the morning to find Selena curled up next to me.

"Hey." I shook her gently. "Wake up."

"Uh… How early is it?"

"Very early. I'm not sure."

"Okay then." She got off the ground and brushed herself off. "Well now since we're up, I wanted to tell you something."

"Alright. What is it?"

"I'll tell you in just a sec. But let me show

you somewhere cool." She led me back down the road toward the giant tree but took a detour left up the mountain.

"Where are we going?" I asked.

"You'll see. Trust me. So, on the thing I was going to tell you. Did you see this brown haired girl, with misty eyes and a permanent scowl?"

"Yeah. She saved me from a monster yesterday. Although she kind of scares me."

I met her yesterday. She came with Daniel and James with her friend Rowen. She's always super rough and stuff,which is basically the opposite of her friend. But that's not the important part. But first, have you ever tried to control mist, or something else?"

"No," I answered. "I've never tried. But I don't think I can."

"Yeah. You're an elemental. But you can only control the four main elements: earth, air, fire, and water. You have been able to cast ice spells and other things, but not very well." I nodded and said, "So is this girl an improved elemental, or what?"

"Basically. She's actually a daughter of Alluvion, but she can control all elements perfectly. It's crazy. And the worst part is, she might just be related to you." I frowned. "So I'm not the most powerful demigod in the world anymore? And I'm just not going to ask about this related-to-me thing."

"You sound crestfallen. Oh! Here we are!"

143

We had been going uphill through forested land, but we now reached a large flat area scattered with rocks. A crystal clear lake stood right to the left, clean of any ripples. The view was incredible.

"Wow," I said. "This place is amazing. And-" I noticed two people climbing a large boulder sitting in the middle of the plateau. "Who are they?"

"Will? Selena?" one of the figures called. "Is that you?"

"Yeah," I responded. "Who are you?"

"I'm Sarah. And Yohan's behind me."

"Cool." We headed closer until we were right next to them. "Why'd you come here?" She shrugged. "Nice view, I guess. And, I had a weird feeling about this place. It's the conjunction of all the elements."

"How?" Selena said.

"Well, we have Earth beneath us, we're high up in the sky, there's a lake right here, and I can sense magma underneath the surface."

"Interesting."

"I feel like this is where we're going to have our final stand. This will be where either Oblivion destroys us, or we destroy him." *Final stand.* The words echoed through my mind.

"Well, that's nice to know," I grumbled. The bushes back down near the path rustled. I instinctively raised Malachite. We advanced to the target.

"Who's there?" I called.

"-Stupid!" a squeaky voice complained. Two people burst out onto the clearing.

One was the girl who had saved me last time when I was thrown into the crater. She was wearing a white tank top and jeans under a thick overcoat and wielded a Swiss Army knife. Weird. The other person was a guy, and he was definitely albino. His thick hair was sprayed all over his head and was sticking in a million directions like a mad scientist, and his eyes looked just like Selena's. He had on a beach shirt and shorts, like he just visited Hawaii, and was as skinny as a wire.

"Who are you?" the girl demanded in a disgusted tone. "And why are you trying to skewer me with that weird lumpy knife?" I lowered Malachite.

"Actually," I corrected. "Who are you?"

"Um… I'm Rowen," he said in a small voice. "She's Kamryn. Also known as Kam."

"Kam?" Selena squeaked. "So you're-"

"Why do you look so surprised?" I demanded. "You-" She shot me a look that told me to shut up.

"Speak up, boy!" Kam ordered. "They can't hear you! As you can see, this guy is my friend, and he's the son of a rich guy. Then some weird people appeared to our cruise ship and-"

"Wait, hold up!" Selena said.

"And then I summoned this dragon dude-"

"Hold on!"

"-and he flew-"

"Quiet!" she thundered. "I already know!" If anyone could deal with this peculiar Kam person, it was Selena.

"Okay, okay," the girl mumbled. "I'll retell it, if you didn't understand it the first time."

"No! Wait! You need us to introduce ourselves too?" she said. "Or are you the star of the show?"

"Of course I'm the star," Kam argued, gaining her confidence once again. "You want to fight?"

"Sure."

"Hey!" Rowen yelped. "Stop it!"

"Out of my way, boy," Kam said, shoving him aside. "This isn't your business right now." I stepped back. Even if this person could control all the elements, I was sure that Selena had more experience in battle. She readied her wind blade, while the other held up her dagger.

Selena quickly slashed, sidestepped an attack, slashed, sidestepped, and knocked the knife out of her hand. Kam cried, "HEY!" A hunk of rock shifted out of the ground and blasted Selena back at least twenty yards.

"Okay, okay!" I said, stepping in. "You win, okay? Now we really to talk." A gust of wind rushed through and blasted her off her feet.

"Now it's on!" she growled.

"STOP! Selena, you stop too! Get over here!" She stomped over, and I had to grab her arm to restrain her from doing anything again.

"Okay," Sarah said. "I'm Sarah, this here is my friend Yohan, and they're Selena and Will. Don't call him William."

"Sure. I don't care. Hi William. Now on with my story." She talked about how Rowen had invited her on a ship sailing across the Atlantic, but a huge storm whipped up. The twins with "black magic, or green magic" as Kam called it had come to save them. Apparently Rowen fought with a massive wind battleaxe, and Kam fought with her magical Swiss Army knife.

"Who's your parents?" I asked. Kam's eyes got even mistier, or maybe I was just seeing things.

"My mom died a year ago in a… never mind. Apparently my dad some old crusty god called Alluvion. By the way, doesn't Alluvion sound like a shampoo?"

"Selena uses cinnamon shampoo," I muttered under my breath.

"What?"

So, we continued talking, got into a few arguments about whether chocolate or vanilla ice cream is better (vanilla, definitely) and also about whether dogs or llamas are better (that was a hard choice, but I like llamas).

    Anyways, that was that.

Chapter 9

After Kam and Rowen had left back through the trees (Kam said that she liked to take the hard path), Sarah sighed and said, "That was weird."

"She's annoying," Selena grumbled.

"You don't like anyone who can beat you up, huh?" I asked.

"Well, no! Yes! No! I mean... she didn't beat me up! And I'm going to beat you into a pulp if you don't stop." I raised my hands in surrender. "Okay then. I got it."

"We better get going, though," Yohan suggested. "I have a feeling that today's gonna be a big day." We all nodded in agreement and then headed down the hill towards the battle.

When we finally got down to the path, things weren't going well. The monster army was already fighting and had pushed all the way down near Crystal Cave, our evacuation site.

Kam was fighting like a monster with her blade, slashing through multiple enemies at once. She occasionally blasted random types of energy, sometimes earth energy, sometimes ice, sometimes mist.

The Grovites had all started chanting a spell. Roots spurted from the ground and started tangling monsters. Green magic filled the air and then was released into the army.

Since I was stuck in the back of the front lines, I started lobbing Malachite's sword projectiles over people's heads. Behind me, Now my weapon glowed fainted red and throbbed like a beating heart. That probably wasn't a good sign.

Soon we were pushed back to Moro Rock. Some monsters turned and started to climb up the tight, winding pathway to the top. I had no idea why they were doing it. Maybe they were sightseeing.

Surprisingly, there weren't any tourists around, though I expected some to be here still. Perhaps they all were evacuated, to where, I don't know, because most of the outside world was in the process of being destroyed too.

"All good?" Selena said, coming right up next to me.

"Yeah."

"Okay. You were staring off into the distance or something. But here's the scary part. We're approaching the tree. Some Grovite enchanters put a barrier around the area, but I'm not sure if it's going to hold."

"Is it easy ground to fight on, at least?"

"I don't know. There's a winding path that leads downhill to a large flat area. If you don't walk on the path, you risk tumbling down the slope. Hopefully we can still funnel the monsters like we're doing now."

Sadly, we couldn't funnel the monsters. As soon as we reached the place where the path led downhill, the monsters sprayed out in a bunch of directions and started charging down the hill.

I faced a giant that was barreling straight at me and ducked under his heavy armor. He grunted, confused, but was soon reduced to a pile of ashes.

Ten warriors charged straight at me. I destroyed three of them with one swipe of my dagger, blew up two more by firing elemental energy. The remaining five glowered at me and charged with their rapiers pointed and ready to strike.

Quickly, I swiped one of their weapons out of their hand and stuck the guy in the chest. He dissolved into ashes, which I blew all over the place to fluster the monsters. While they were coughing, Malachite's projectiles came in and did the work for me. Now there was only one left.

"Your hope is useless!" he growled. "No need to fight!"

"I've been told that a million times today!" I answered. He grinned and kicked me in the stomach while I was distracted, and I went tumbling down the steep slope.

"Hey!" I cried. "Ow! Stop! No!" I knocked my head on a million things while rolling down the hill, and I finally came to a stop at the base of the big tree.

"Will! You okay?" Selena rushed up to me and knelt down next to me.

"I'm... I'm fine-"

"Oh no!" Kam jeered. "Poor William got hurt! He got a little boo-boo!"

"Shut up!" Selena snapped. "Go help fight the battle or do something useful, idiot!"

"Sure, mom, thanks for telling me what to do," she said and ran off.

"Kam's weird," I said. "Just ignore her." Selena held out her hand and helped me up.

"You're welcome," she said. "Now go off and fight. Don't get hurt." I smiled and turned just in time to face an Oblivion monster glowing with blue runes.

"Aaah!" I screamed. He zipped by me with extraordinary speed and came back again as a red blur with his spear pointed right at me. I just managed to deflect his swing, but he was already back for another round.

"Who are you?" I gasped.

"Just a warrior. With speed runes. Impossible to kill." He stopped for a second. "Alumenta is powering us. If she gets destroyed, all rune power is gone. Soon, every warrior here will have the ability to move like the wind, and-" He stopped and stared down at the arrow embedded in his chest.

"Whoops," I muttered. "Maybe not impossible to kill." But in my heart, I was really worried about this soldier with amazing agility. If every monster in the army had speed, they would be indestructible.

I rushed over to where Selena was battling a horde of giants. Making quick work of the last one, she looked at me, and I told her what had happened.

"Oh no. The worst thing that could happen would be Alumenta going over to the enemy's side. I hope that doesn't happen."

"William!" Kam exclaimed. She jogged down next to us. "Oblivion is hiking up Moro Rock right now for unknown reasons! Get your butt over there and find out what he's doing!"

"Why don't you find out?" I demanded. "Are we your personal servants or what?"

"Yes you are! Now go! Once he's separated from the rest of the army, you might have a chance of beating him!"

...

There Oblivion stood, in all his glory at the peak of the rock wearing a weird billowing black cape. To reach him, we had to cross a narrow passage across the top of the slab to a landing that had a bunch of signs on it telling a bunch of junk like how the rock's passage was built and a lot of other mumbo jumbo.

The lord of the abyss tore the sign out of the

ground with his bare hands and hurled it over the edge.

"Why is he here?" I whispered.

"I dunno. My guess is that this rock signifies solitude, which is basically the opposite of the void."

"Or maybe he's just sightseeing."

"I doubt that. Hey, weren't there other monsters who were coming up here? Where'd they go?"

"Oh. We may have just gotten ourselves into a trap." Oblivion turned around and smiled wickedly with David's face. "Oh yes you have." I whipped around behind us. Twenty elite warriors popped out from behind the rocks.

"I'm surprised at how stupid you were just to come up here," he said. "I expected more from you."

"Wait. So you mean Kam tricked us?"

"Kam? That disgusting girl? Oh no. She was perfectly honest. But I'm very disappointed that you fell for my little trick. Well, then, enough chat. Let's get into action." He raised his hand and grabbed a long broadsword from the air. I held up Malachite, willing it to extend to its full length.

Immediately, Oblivion swung his claymore at me. I tried to block it. Malachite rumbled and hissed as his blade deflected off mine.

"Ha! Your poor legendary weapon won't

stand a chance against me." Swinging again, he slashed a giant cut through my stomach. It didn't go far, but it still hurt like crazy.

Behind me, Selena was blasting the monsters with air, sometimes stepping in for the kill. Hopefully she would survive their assault and turn back to help me.

I had to focus on my battle, not hers. The sword came back again, and I ducked.

Think, I told myself. *I have to do this. For my family. For my friends. For Hannah. For Connor.*

"Get away!" I screamed. A ripple of energy surged out from me. Oblivion stumbled for a moment but laughed. "You stand no chance, puny demigod. Surrender." Anger and rage boiled in my stomach.

"NO!" I shot forward, blasting elemental energy, swinging Malachite, launching spells from my spell tome.

"Whoa!" I startled Oblivion so bad that David started talking again. "What? Will-"

"Shut up!" Oblivion growled. He lifted his sword to attack, but it was knocked out of his hand by Malachite.

"Hey-" A beam of energy hit his face. "Ahh!" Blast after blast of magic hit him until he was pushed to the edge of the railing.

"Get out of David's body!" I said.

"No! No!" I drew back my foot and kicked

him over the edge.

Okay. I'm not even sure what I was thinking there. Obviously, Oblivion would not get defeated that way, so I got punished for that.

There I stood, thinking I was the coolest guy in the world, standing on that high peak of the rock when my enemy materialized right behind me. The butt of his blade jutted into my back, and down the cliff I went.

"HELP!" I screeched. "No!" I grabbed desperately for any handholds and finally found one right before I plunged to my death.

Above me, Selena was trying to defend against Oblivion while I hoisted myself back up to the top.

"This ends now!" Oblivion yelled. He raised his hand and started rapid-fire bombarding us with fireball after fireball.

"Duck!" She pulled me to the ground, a projectile narrowly missing my head. Rain started pouring onto our heads, completely drenching us.

"Away!" he roared. A red forcefield enveloped him and exploded blasting us back to the edge of the rock. "You'll never win!"

"Quiet!" I snapped, firing more spells. "I've now heard that a billion times today!"

Oblivion stomped his foot, and another ripple of energy came out.

"Will!" Selena screamed. "Use what the

water person told you! Whatever it was!" I nodded and remembered. *Think happy thoughts.* With a loud crash, the flat of Oblivion's claymore came down onto my poor friend's head. She crumpled onto the ground.

So I thought happy thoughts. I thought about all those times when I sat with my friends around the lake, eating dinner, watching the sunset. A strange golden glow surrounded me. Oblivion winced and stumbled back.

Did I do it? I thought, losing my concentration. The glow dissipated, and Oblivion threw back his head and laughed.

"You can't defeat me!"

"Maybe I can!" I continued to remember when we had our sniper battle and won, when Abaddon cleansed the Corruption, when I enjoyed my birthday with my mom and Zach.

My eyes stung. My head throbbed. I wanted to sink into a bed and go into a heavy slumber forever.

Around me, I faintly noticed the brilliant white beams that were shooting from me and that they were rapidly growing hotter.

"Ahh!" David said, his voice coming back and taking hold of his body. His black, lifeless eyes blinked and turned back to normal. "Will. Stop-"

"Oh, shut up, idiot!" Oblivion screeched. "I will not fail now! Back-" He fell to the ground.

"I- I can't... hold any longer," I cried. "Someone! Please!"

"Shoot it at me!" Selena said.

"What?"

"You don't have enough power to destroy Oblivion completely! But you can transfer his spirit!"

"I won't. No way."

"Please," she begged. Right now's not the time for decisions. You're going to black out soon." It was true. Yellows spots danced before my sight. The glow died down almost completely.

"Why?"

"I... I think I can control him. I can annoy him from the inside. I'll be fine. Please."

"No," I said, but I did it. Quickly, I gave her a hug, quite possibly the last hug I would ever give to her.

Focusing all my power and will on David, I wrenched the spirit out of him and cast it at Selena.

Her eyes dimmed and turned pure black.

"No..."

...

I felt like my brain was removed from my head, bashed on by three hundred Solarians, and finally incinerated by solar rays.

(Maybe my brain had been incinerated by

solar rays, judging from the beams of light coming out of me and the fact that everywhere around me was melted into magma).

"Oh… geez," I moaned. "What just happened?" Around me, a ring of slowly-cooling lava had formed, and a few people had been surveying the destruction.

"Stay down," Sarah whispered. She seemed to be crouched behind me. "Here's a cool cloth." She laid it on my forehead, and I closed my eyes again.

"Where's… where's Selena? And David?" No answer came.

"Um… Will. Just rest. You'll be up in no time."

I had a horrible nightmare about evil flying ponies, a possessed puppy, and dripping magma. Other than that, I was fine and woke up again.

"Hey Will." Yohan stood above me, his eyes red, like he had just cried. I stood up and felt a bit dizzy. Remembering all those times when I had used Selena as a crutch, a pang of sadness echoed through my heart. "David wants to see you."

"Oh!" I squeaked. My voice sounded a few octaves higher than usual. "Is he okay?"

"Well…" We headed back down Moro Rock to a flat area covered with grass and shrubbery. David was lying flat on the ground. His lips were cracked and bleeding.

"Hi," I said. In my mind, I wasn't really sure what to say, since he'd just been possessed by the worst guy in the world. "Um… how did it feel to be trapped in his body? Was it painful? Or…"

"It felt like being trapped in an endless black prison. And I couldn't see anything. But when Oblivion lost power, I was sort of back to my normal body. It's hard to explain."

"You'll be okay, right? Is-" He shook his head and winced. "Sorry Will. He pushed me to the max. I can't. Where's Hannah?" Yohan tapped my shoulder and told me that they hadn't told David yet.

"She's… she's gone."

"Okay. I'll see her up in… wherever, hopefully. Thanks." He closed his eyes and took a shaky breath.

"All right." I stood up and walked away to Sarah, who was half crying. "What happened to the rest of the army?"

"They retreated after they saw that Oblivion had taken a new body. He needs time to get adjusted, and that's also why he wanted to leave right after he took David's body. And, about our group. I was thinking. We started with so many people. Now, it's only you, me, and Yohan."

"Well, that's depressing."

"Yeah." She wiped away some tears from her face. "Is it okay if you go away for a bit? Sorry. I need some time by myself right now."

"Okay. I'll go." Turning, I shuffled away and decided to sulk behind a tree next to the cliff. How wonderful.

Again, the sun was dipping behind the tall mountains. *That's the end of the twenty-seventh,* I thought. *We need to head back to Abyssion to do whatever he needs.*

HI! Darkecho's great head peered at me from below. *Why're you crying? Do you have brownies? Where're the blondies? I want to eat them!*

"Um… hi," I muttered. "What do you need?"

You seem sad. You want me to take you for a fly?

"Yeah," I answered. "That would be great."

Okay then. Hop on. He flew up, and I mounted on his back. *Let's go!* We soared into the sky, the wind whipping into our faces.

"So, Darkecho."

Yeah?

"Abyssion needs us for some mission at Aquaia's fortress. We need to head back to Oceanside Pier."

Back to that yucky place? So claustrophobic. There's no room to fly anywhere!

"Yeah. Sorry. We have to go back there."

Chapter 10

Here we are, peeps! Darkecho exclaimed. The moon was just rising above the clear night sky as I surveyed the destruction of the tsunami below us.

"Goodness," Sarah grumbled. "It's worse than I expected." My dragon landed down at the partially wrecked pier, startling a few police officers (maybe they thought that Darkecho was a very oversized pigeon).

"I can go down alone," I suggested quietly. "Because you're both fire people. You won't fare well down there."

"No," Yohan responded. "We have to go with you."

"Yeah," Sarah agreed. "We'll be fine."

"Uh… Yohan? Remember that time when we were at Yharon's jungle last year? How you were getting soaked in the rain?"

"I remember." He winced. "It was not fun."

Guys? Time's wasting here. You better decide soon.

"We have decided," Sarah declared. "We're all going! Right, Will?" She glared at me.

"Right," I mumbled glumly.

"Hey?" She patted my back. "What's

wrong?"

"Nothing. Just… worrying. About Selena." I felt like if I talked anymore, I would burst into tears.

"She'll be fine. I promise."

"But… what if she has the same fate as David? I mean-"

"Don't think that way!" Sarah scolded. "Don't worry about what might happen, focus on what's happening right now."

"Okay then."

"Let's go."

We hopped into the murky water and disappeared beneath the depths (I think some bystanders saw us).

When we came out the other side, the first thing I realized was that there was no water.

"What?" I squeaked. "What? No!" The next thing I saw was a huge dark shape hurtling at us.

I'll catch you! Darkecho yelled. With a thump, we were all on his back again. *Never mind. This place is very roomy. Lots of places to fly- Gah!* A white beam of light shot out from somewhere below, and he swerved dangerously.

"Fly down!" I commanded. "Hopefully they won't hit us." Slowly but surely, we descended down to the front wall of the fortress, which was somehow still holding up.

"You've come here, eh?" Abyssion said. He was now at least fifteen feet tall, with glowing eyes and horrendously ugly hair sticking up in a million directions. "Good. As you can tell, all the water started to evaporate after you left. I sucked it back up into my bottle."

"So?"

"I detected this weird stone in the enemy camp, and I think that it's the cause of the water disappearing."

"That's great," I responded. "Now who should go?"

"I dunno." He shrugged. "Two of you. I need one of you to help with this protection. Also, beware of the krakens."

"Krakens?"

"Have you not heard of them?" I remembered a hazy memory of Selena telling me about sea monsters before I got thrown into the lake. That was horrifying.

"Oh. I see."

"I'll go!" Yohan volunteered. "Sarah can stay here."

"And miss out on all the action? No thank you." Abyssion rolled his eyes and said, "You people can figure it out. The rock is yellow. Bye." He disappeared in a blast of briny water.

"The rock is yellow," I repeated. "Great. Not helpful at all."

"Well, it gives us some hint about what it is. That's something," Yohan said. "We better go.

Bye!"

"Wait-"

But we were already gone.

...

"So, to get to the enemy's base, we have to go past those huge piles of rocks, through that pit that leads to who knows where, over the ravine, and up the hill," I explained. "Simple."

"Got it." Yohan seemed paler than usual. The embers in his eyes flickered weakly.

At the piles of boulders, we met our first enemy. A sea green creature with tentacles and a huge gaping mouth was aimlessly gliding through the area, occasionally shooting blasts of toxic water at the rubble.

"Is that a kraken?" I whispered, crouching.

"Yeah. I think he's an enemy."

"Great. What do we do?"

"Sneak around?" he suggested. "I don't know."

"Okay then. Very quiet-" I stepped back and tripped. The kraken whipped around, focusing its one huge eyeball straight at us.

"Duck!" Yohan yelled, right as it launched a high-intensity blue laser at me. Luckily, its aim was a bit off, or I would have been a pile of burnt meat.

"Flank him!" I said. "You go from the front, I

go from the back!"

"Can you go from the front?" Yohan complained, but he did it. I crept around the colorful coral pillars and arrived at the back of the monster. Suddenly, Yohan cried out in pain.

"What?" I murmured, peering at the kraken. It had knocked him down onto the ground and was preparing to fire a laser.

"Yaaah!" I screamed and knocked him aside just as the beast fired his beam. "Die!" I hacked at his skin and ended up dislocating my arm. "Ow! Ow!"

"Hide!" Yohan said. "I'll take care of it!" He raised his blade and fended it off for a bit. Behind a rock, I mumbled the healing spell, half blinded by the pain.

"Coming!" I yelled and crawled out to face the monster. "How do we destroy it?"

"The mouth!" He blocked a blast of salt water. "Everywhere else is armored!"

"How do we get it to open its mouth? What if it has bad breath?" The kraken slammed against Yohan, and he went flying.

"Hey!" I called, waving my hands. "Ugly! Get over here!" It roared, and I nearly fainted of the unmistakable scent of dead, rotten fish and rancid sewer water.

"Too slow to get me, huh? Come get me!" I bumped against the back of a mountainous coral reef and started to climb.

"Go Will!" Yohan cheered. Big mistake. The beast turned his foul head toward him and spat a blast of seawater at him. He toppled over and hit the ground unconscious.

"Oh, jeez," I mumbled. "Hopefully he'll be fine." I had to get its attention again, or it would eat Yohan. "Hey, idiot! Get here, stinky face!" He didn't even turn at me. Drawing my bow, I aimed it at it and fired at his metallic behind.

Of course, it did no damage, but he now regarded me as another target to devour.

"Open wide!" I said. "C'mon, buddy!" The kraken gave a confused growl, like a puppy. My head formulated a slightly risky plan as I arrived at the top of the hunk of coral.

So maybe he can understand English, I thought. *I could persuade him to open his mouth and-* Downstairs, it roared and jolted me out of my thinking.

"Yikes!" I squeaked and fell down a hole. It took me several moments to get out, and I hoped that he didn't lose interest in me. Luckily, he was still waiting for me at the base of the rock. "Open up! I thought you had something stuck in your tooth!"

"Rrrr?" It cocked its head at me and whimpered.

"Okay buddy." I really didn't want to destroy

it now. "Just stay calm, and I'll come down." And as soon as I arrived back down at the bottom, he switched from cute doggie mode to scary kraken mode again.

He spit a blast of water at me, smashing me into a boulder. My back exploded in pain. Spots danced before my eyes.

"Easy," I mumbled weakly. "Stop." The monster floated close to me and started a laser beam blast. "No, doggie. Please."

"Die!" Yohan leaped from a rock and landed on top of the beast.

"Grrrrr!" He shook and opened his wide mouth. That was my chance. I threw Malachite like a throwing dagger straight into his giant maw.

"Hhh-ack." It made a sound like a clogged faucet (trust me, I've handled that multiple times) and burst into water and some other sea plants.

"Gross," Yohan muttered, peeling a slab of seaweed off his back. "But that was pretty awesome."

"Awesome? You were awesome. You saved my life." I gazed out into the distance, avoiding eye contact with him.

"What's wrong? Are you thinking about Selena again?"

"Huh? Oh." My face turned crimson. "No. I just kind of feel bad destroying that kraken. He was sort of cute."

"I'm sure Santa will give you another baby kraken for Christmas."

"Yeah, sure." We forged ahead.

...

And next up was the huge pit of doom.

There wasn't any efficient way to get across, so we decided just to head into it and come out the other side.

That was a crummy choice.

Inside the pit, it was so dark that we couldn't see anything (and Yohan's powers were definitely not working) and the ground was peppered with sharp, jagged rocks and tangling kelp.

"Not fun!" I said. "Ahh!" My foot slipped on a rock, and down the depression I went, crashing into boulders and getting scratched by little pieces of the ground.

Finally, I came to a stop at the bottom of the pit, where you could barely see a foot in front of you.

"Will!" Yohan's voice echoed through the valley. "Where are you?"

"I don't know! Somewhere down here!" I felt something brush against my shoulder.

"Try walking somewhere!" he said.

"No! I'll just wait for you here! You can find me! Or I'll find you!"

"You can find me!"

"Okay!" I started wandering throughout the hole, looking for him again. Out of nowhere, an Oblivion monster popped out.

"AHH!" I squeaked, falling back. "Who… who are you?"

"Hmm? Hey! Someone else! I've been lost in this place for… ten years or so. But now you can help me find my way out, right?"

"Ten years?"

"Pretty much. Or maybe thirty years. I've lost track."

"And you couldn't find your way out?"

"Nope! I kept walking in one direction, but I never came out. It's been lonely down here, though. You are a friend of Oblivion, no?"

"Uh…' I didn't respond, because my tiny brain cells were at hard work.

Ten years? What if we're stuck in here for ten years? What if I never get to see any of my friends- No. I can't think this way. Just like Sarah said. Ignore what might happen. Pay attention to what's happening right now.

"Hello, person!" He rapped on my skull with his knuckles. "Are you alive? I'm talking to you!"

"Huh? Yeah. I'm alive. Sure."

"So, are you a friend of Oblivion?"

"Oblivion's bad. Don't follow him. He's going to destroy the world." That sounded pretty

170

stupid.

"Pffft! We like destruction! But if you're not a friend, then I guess I have to stick you with my spear. Oh well. I wanted a friend." He prepared to strike.

"No!" I deflected his swing with Malachite and slashed a huge welt in his mask.

He was surprisingly agile for a guy who was stuck in a hole for a decade, and he soon told me why. "I was the head general of Oblivion's army. Gave him advice and feedback. Almost defeated Aer. But then they sent me down to this horrible ocean to battle. Totally wasting their troops."

"Great!" I sidestepped right into his lance, which caught me on my thigh. "OW! No!"

"See. I told you. You don't stand a chance."

"NO!" A wave of energy rushed out from me and turned him into a pile of dust.

"Take that," I mumbled. Yohan appeared in the distance and rushed to me.

"What happened?"

"Ow. Something happened. Heal… please."

"Okay. Quick. Where's your spell tome?"

"In my backpack. Quick. It really hurts." Tears welled up in my eyes because of the pain.

Soon, I was back to normal again, and I told him about what had happened. He shuddered. "That does not sound fun. But we will be able to leave here, won't we?"

"Let's hope we can."

"Sarah will be very mad if we don't make it out of here." So we started trudging through the endless mist.

It felt like we had just walked a marathon when we broke out of the fog and arrived at the other side of the valley. My legs were feeling even worse than the time we went hiking in Sequoia.

"Thank goodness," I moaned. "That we are out of that stupid place. But next up we have another ravine. Let's not go into this one." The chasm was at least thirty feet across, definitely not jumpable.

"Yes, please," he agreed. "Then how do we get across?"

"Uh… We go around it?" The gaping slash across the earth stretched at least a mile in each direction, the ends not visible to us.

"Maybe not. Can you summon in some kind of bridge? You are an elemental."

"I can't. Sorry."

"Then…" He scratched at his chin. "I guess we have to go down and back up."

Did I regret that choice? Most definitely. I'd rather walk around the ravine (though Abyssion later told me that it was fifty miles worth of walking to get around it).

Luckily, it was only about a two-story climb down and back up, and there were many handholds.

Gradually, we made our way down, sometimes slipping. Once, I lost my grip on a piece of slippery moss and almost fell down. Fortunately, I found a handhold (which unfortunately was Yohan's blond hair).

"Ow!" He lost his balance and almost fell the rest of the ten feet to the bottom.

We were done with that last obstacle and finally to the camp. By then, I was about to pass out from fatigue and thirstiness (very ironic, since we were in an ocean).

"Finally… here," I wheezed. "Let's sleep, please."

"C'mon," Yohan urged. "Just a little bit more."

"Last time we snuck into a camp, it didn't go well. I think we almost blew up the whole mountain."

"Well, then, what can go wrong here? There aren't any mountains to blow up. Let's go!"

We arrived at the outskirts of the base, which was not ringed by monsters.

"Great," I muttered. "What do we do now? Check in every single tent to see if there's a yellow stone in it?"

"We could. But I sense this force in here. It's drawing me toward it. I think… aha!" He pointed his finger to the least conspicuous place of them all: a tiny rundown shack near the edge of the place.

But the only guards around were situated around it. How odd.

"Agreed." I nodded. "How do we get in there, anyway?"

"Runes?"

"No way." I shuddered. "Some Oblivion monsters have this insane speed boost, and we're not sure if Alumenta has headed to the enemy side or what. That's also another thing to put on our checklist: check on her."

"Great. So, just charge?"

"Yeah. Selena-" I paused for a moment. "Selena would not approve. But let's go."

We launched ourselves at the few guards. I cut one of them in half, and immediately an alarm sounded.

"What? How? Quick! We need to get in before reinforcements arrive!"

"Yes please!" I threw open the door to the building, and I didn't know what to expect. Instead of the inside of a room, there was a tunnel made out of steel leading downward.

"Interesting," I said. "Where is it?" I bolted the door behind me, and we rushed down the passage to a vaulted door.

"Yah!" I threw Malachite at the gateway, and it exploded into metal pieces. We finally arrived at another room layered with wires.

"Oh no," Yohan mumbled. "Tripwires. I

hope you're good at limbo." He ducked under the first cord and made his way across the room to the other side.

"You get the stone!" I called. "I'll stay here! Maybe fend off some monsters!"

"Okay! Bye!" He disappeared into the next room, and I turned to face the horde of monsters ready to annihilate me.

A stream of monsters started coming in, me slaying them one by one but them pushing me closer and closer to the trap. Finally, I toppled back and hit about a hundred wires.

The enemies all stormed on top of me falling on top of me, getting hit by various assorts of poisoned arrows and jabbed by spears from above.

Soon, they were mostly dispersed, and only a few remained, and they all retreated back outside, perhaps waiting for more reinforcements.

It felt like an eternity before Yohan came out again, holding a shining neon yellow stone in his hand.

"All good?" he asked.

"Yeah. They all got destroyed on the traps. We need to leave because more monsters are coming soon."

"Let's go. It's a long way back."

...

So, how did we get back? Well, Sarah was waiting for us at the ravine with her arms crossed and her foot tapping.

"What took you so long?" she snapped. "I've been waiting for at least an hour now!"

"Uh… we just got stuck in a pit of no return and went on a very difficult rock climb," Yohan said. "And what about you?"

"I just made a bridge over the ravine, and I went around the pit. It was pretty easy."

"That's great," I mumbled. "Well, we took the hard path." Sarah threw her arms around Yohan. "I'm just so glad that you actually survived. With this guy guiding you, I kind of doubted it."

"Oh, shut up. Now let's get back, shall we?"

After a very lengthy trek back to Aquaia's fortress (and Abyssion was still holding up the front wall), we climbed up to his tower where he was waiting.

"Excuse me!" he growled. "I told one of you to stay with me! Do you not understand English, or are you not good at following directions?"

"She's not good at following directions," Yohan muttered. Sarah hit his arm. That's the normal friend relationship we have here, you see?

"Okay, then, blond girl. Next time, learn to follow directions. Anyway, can I see the rock?"

"Bring it out," I said. He took the yellow pebble from his pocket and placed it in his hand.

"Hmm." Abyssion examined it and turned it over. "Seems like... uranium. Highly radioactive uranium infused with some sort of water repelling substance."

"What?" Yohan shrieked, nearly bursting my eardrums. "I just had in my pocket for a long time! What if-"

"You'll be fine," he said. "I just scan you." He waved his hand over Yohan's body and nodded. "No radioactivity. But I need to take this rock up to the surface and give it to some scientists. I believe I know of some down in UC San Diego somewhere. It'll be a good treat for them."

"And carry it again?" Sarah growled. "No thank you."

"Oh, honey." Abyssion made a tsk-tsk sound and tried to stroke her hair. She swatted his hand aside. "You really must learn to respect the gods. Treat them the same way you treat your relatives, for instance."

"One of my relatives is Yharon. I treat him about the same way I treat you! My father is John Miller. I resent him."

"What about your mom, hmm?" As he saw Sarah's face darken, he immediately continued talking. "She died. Oh poor blond girl. Lost her mommy." Man, Abyssion knew how to get into people's nerves.

"Well, then. It's time to go. Here's your rock.

Bring it to those professors. I believe your dragon has flown up to the surface because the air ventilation in here is poor. Goodbye."

Chapter 11

He waved his hand, and we were back at the Oceanside Pier. The moon was only at its peak right now, which kind of surprised me. I was fairly certain that we were stuck in that valley for a good day or so.

"Ugh!" Sarah stomped her foot on the creaking wooden boards. "I hate that Abyssion. And I don't think I'll be hugging radioactive Yohan for a while."

"What do we do with this thing?" Yohan held it up in his hand.

"Throw it back in the ocean!" she cried. "Who cares about Abyssion and his stupid battle?" I hadn't seen her in such a terrible condition since we witnessed Betsy her mother away. She usually acted like a second mom to me.

"Hey!" I said. "Calm down. I know that Abyssion is annoying, but we can't just throw this rock into the ocean."

"Calm down? Why should I calm down? Abyssion's a monster!"

"Please."

"Sorry. Just the mention of my mom. It…" She buried her head in Yohan's shoulder and started sobbing.

BLONDIES! Darkecho swooped from the air

and landed on the pier, nearly splintering it under his weight. *And a yellow rock! Can I eat it?*

"Uh… Darkecho. You can't eat it. It's radioactive. And we're talking right now. Could you find something else to do?"

Darkecho cocked his head. *What?* He spotted Sarah. *Okay. Okay. I'll chase some squirrels, then. Bye!* He flew away, accidentally smashed down the peak of a skyscraper, and started gliding after a helicopter.

"Jeez," I mumbled. "What is he doing?" I wasn't exactly sure what to do now, because I was pretty sure that Yohan had the situation under control.

"Look. It'll be fine," Yohan comforted. "Don't worry."

"Yeah. I will. Sorry." She lowered her gaze.

"Hey!" I said. "It's nothing to be ashamed about. Seriously. I cry about stuff all the time."

"Okay. Sorry. Call Darkecho down. We should go and drop this stone off to those people quickly and head to Alumenta after."

"Sure."

Little did we know that dropping that stone off would be a huge pain in the neck.

...

A few moments later, Darkecho dropped us

in a dark street with a sign that said Pangea Drive.

"They spelled it wrong," Sarah pointed out.

"Smartypants."

A brick wall blocking a row of fancy homes lined the right sidewalk, and all we saw on the left were a bunch of pine trees and bushes.

"Those are Torrey Pine trees. Some high school person did research on it and earned a whole bunch of money."

"So?"

Sarah shrugged. "Just sayin'. So where's this UC San Diego thing he was talking about?"

"Forward." Yohan pointed to a sign reading *Muir College - University of California San Diego*.

"Then won't it be a huge place?" Sarah wondered. "Who do we give it to? Why is Abyssion so stupid?" I myself had those questions too but decided not to say so.

"Well, we better take a look, then."

The road curved left, and we entered an expansive parking lot with looming buildings in the background. A stone skyscraper stood on the right with illuminated windows, and some other ugly buildings were in the distance on the left, partially blocked by an assortment of pipes.

But the whole place was brimming with Oblivion monsters.

"Oh, jeez. Let's get in the bushes." We crouched low, watching them swarm around the area like ants, sitting on cars and pretty much trashing the whole place.

"What?" Sarah said. "Are the people okay? Maybe Abyssion sent us here not just for bringing the rock."

"Okay," I whispered. "Here's the plan. We should go through the bushes to that clump of ugly buildings." I pointed at the ones on the left. "Sneak behind those weird tubes and get to the ugly building there." I pointed at the tall stone structure.

"Maybe there are people in there."

"Yeah. That's why. Let's go." We weaved through the bushes and arrived at the place where we had to dash across to the pipes.

"Three, two, one, go!" Sarah and Yohan raced across the street, but I stayed back because a group of monsters was just walking by. One of them froze. "Did you see that? Two demigods runnin' across the street?"

"You're crazy, man. Let's go before the boss gets us in trouble again." I sprinted across too to join them.

"Did you hear that?" Sarah said. "They have a boss. But let's not worry about that. We need to get over there."

"Yeah." After a few close calls, we were finally to the entrance of the building.

It was actually two separate buildings, connected by an assortment of vine-covered bridges.

We turned to the glass door and tried to open it. It was locked shut.

"Hey!" I pounded on it. "Let us in!" A guy peered out from inside, and his eyes lit up. He swung the door open, and we stepped in.

Inside, it wasn't much prettier. The floor was made out of brown tiles, and the walls were just stone. At least it was warm inside compared to the frigid winds outside.

"Yohan?" he asked. "Is that you?"

"John!"

"Oh man," I said. "It is so nice to meet a friendly face once in a while. So what's going on in here?"

"We have an Aphelist base here, but Oblivion and Cataclysm discovered it. They sent a whole bunch of monsters here, and we're stuck in this building now."

"So what can we do to help?"

"Defeat their leader. He's a huge giant, and he's scouting out the rest of this place right now. Sit down." John patted a bench next to him. Nobody felt like sitting.

"And how the heck did you get stuck in this gloomy place in the first place?" I asked.

"I just came to look around, I guess. I got a distress call from them, telling us to come over and help. So I snuck in, just like you did-"

"How'd you see us?"

"I… uh… I was watching. Anyways, these people swarmed in here, and now we're stuck."

"We have this stupid chunk of rock," Yohan interrupted. "It's highly dangerous… blah, blah, blah, and-"

"Really?" John's eyes suddenly perked up. "Where?"

"In my pocket."

"Because somebody was in the bathroom and found this note hidden in the toilet-"

"Eww." Sarah wrinkled her nose. "Disgusting."

"-and it said that it would fix our problem."

"What is your problem?"

"We have several. One, all the bathrooms have exploded and are flooded after the guy found that note. Two, the whole building is threatening to flood because of that. The person who sent the note said that he would find a rock and send it here."

"Great," Sarah said. "Abyssion used us to give this thing to you. I hate him."

"Abyssion?" John thundered. "Isn't he the one who dropped me into the lake? That's just terrible."

"He is terrible," Sarah agreed. "But oh well, for now. So what do we do?"

"In a few moments, the giant will arrive back again, and he will try to smash the doors open again. By the way, they're charmed. But I'm afraid this time, the door won't hold." In fact, just as he was speaking, the crystal doors shuddered and exploded open.

"Haha!" a deep voice, so deep that it almost broke my ears, growled. "I've finally got in! Now, I destroy everyone!"

And what I saw was so appalling, I don't really want to describe it again.

The giant looked like a regular nine-foot tall person (if nine feet is normal), a really handsome person, actually. He wore a white tunic and pants with a brown belt and satchel under a green cape, kind of like an elf. Even his face looked nice, with a perfect grin and dimples under his cheeks.

But his eyes completely ruined his portrait. They were just full of hate and void, with absolutely no life in them. It was like looking into the deepest part of the Endless Abyss and brought back my worst memories: Oblivion seeping into David's body, Hannah lying on the ground in pain, Connor crouching down and expending his life force to save us, and worst of all, me casting Oblivion's spirit into Selena.

"Who are you?" Sarah demanded in a shaky voice. I whimpered like an anxious cat and hid behind my friends.

"Oh-ho-ho." He laughed, making me think that this was an evil Santa. "I don't want to talk to you. Come out, elemental."

"Yes?" I stepped out from the shadows. "Get out of here. Now." That would have sounded pretty deadly if my legs weren't quaking like a frail doll and my voice wasn't a hoarse whisper.

"I expected more of you," he said. "But all you can do is run away from things. You tried to be brave against all these other foes you have faced. But think! Your brown-haired friend was the one who pinned down Abaddon. You thought you had defeated Yharon, yet Solaria still managed to get the Key of Nightmares and open the chest."

"What-" The void was swirling around me. I felt like sinking into the ground and giving up.

"You did NOTHING to defeat Solaria! Another one of your friends felled her. You are useless, William Hanson. USELESS!" I fell to the ground, tears streaming down my face.

What had I done? I thought. *I didn't do anything. I am useless. I-*

Shut up! The other side of my brain called. *He's just amplifying all the things he's said. Be strong!*

No, no, no. I can't-

"Well, now since that worthless midget is out of the way, it's time for me to conquer the rest of the building!" He marched on, the fog still surrounding me.

"Will!" Somebody shook my head. I opened

one eye and saw Sarah crouched down next to me.

"What?" I mumbled. "I'm useless anyway. Just leave me behind-" She slammed her fist down on a bench so hard that it jolted me completely awake.

"Get. Up," she growled.

"Okay, okay. Sorry."

"That's my good boy." She smiled and ruffled my hair. "By the way, take a shower after we destroy this guy, you're nasty."

...

We discovered the giant (I'm just going to call him Elf Guy) tearing up a classroom down one of the hallways where a bunch of Aphelists were camped.

Fireball after fireball they cast, all of them doing near minimal damage to him.

"What do we do?" I whispered.

"He's all about null and void and nothingness. If you could... I don't know... "out-happy" him, maybe he would be defeated. Or something else. I'm not sure."

"Hey, scaredy-pants!" I called. "Get out here and fight us like a man!" He turned and glared at me with his pitch-black eyes, and I nearly crumpled to the ground again if Sarah hadn't clamped her hand on my shoulder.

"Stay strong," she said in my ear.

"Thanks."

"Here he comes." Elf Guy came flying out of the classroom at full speed and smashed through a row of demigods. Everywhere he looked, people became pale and mist funneled around them.

Up the stairs he went, causing another wave of havoc to seep into the demigods above.

"We need to warn them!" John hissed. "Come! I know another way." We headed into an empty, dark classroom and went through another doorway into a damp passage.

"This is scary," I mumbled. "Let's leave, please."

"C'mon!" Yohan encouraged. "You'll be fine."

"Thanks, man."

"Here we are." John thrust open another door, and we were out on the third-floor walkway.

"How many floors does this place have, anyway?" I said. "I mean, Elf Guy is gonna have a pretty long walk to the top."

"Elf Guy?" Sarah laughed. "Is that what you call him?"

"Well, I guess. He doesn't have a name, does he?"

He shrugged. "I don't know. Now-" A door somewhere near exploded open. "Let's go."

We rushed through the numerous

passageways and warned the people of the coming Elf Guy.

Soon, we had an army of Aphelists at the ready on the second-floor walkway. Sounds of a scuffle came floating out from the stairway, and out came the giant just as he tossed aside one demigod.

"By golly." As he looked over us, waves of fear crashed upon us. "What a crowd I have here, eh?"

Nobody said anything.

"Well, then, that's great. More people to destroy!" He raised the lance he was using for battle and swung it at the Aphelists just as he was bombarded with fireballs.

"Hey!" He flashed his dark eyes across the crowd. "Leave!" Many did as he told.

I decided to take the melee and faced him with Malachite.

"Oh, stop," he said. "Summoning your stupid projectiles from your weapon. You're a coward! Always hiding behind other things!" He forced us up the staircase to the next floor.

Most of the Aphelists ceased firing because they were either hiding or didn't want to waste their energy.

"Is that why you came without any reinforcements? To prove that you're not afraid?"

"Of course!" Elf Guy exclaimed. He swung again, nearly decapitating my head. "I don't need any stupid reinforcements! They're just a hassle to manage. I'm just more powerful by myself."

I looked at the floor number. We were at Floor Three now.

"So you need to prove your worth?" Yohan said.

"Yes... Wait? You don't know my story?"

"Of course we don't, Elf Guy!" I answered. "You're just too ugly to be recognized."

"What?" he roared. "Whatever. Anyways, it was a very long story. I was punished by Oblivion for betraying his side, and I was cast into exile. So I came back to prove my worth!"

"Interesting." I nearly tripped over a potted plant. "And you'll prove your worth by slaughtering a bunch of scared Aphelists? Doesn't sound very noble to me."

"Oh, don't worry. It is noble. I do admire you for your concern." Now we were on the fifth floor. Not good.

"So. Let's sit down and talk, okay?" I persuaded. "Okay?"

"Oh, stop stalling!" he scoffed. "You just don't want to witness my great victory!"

"No, no." I somehow almost fell over another fern. Maybe Zach had donated some of his clumsiness to me. "I just wanted to talk about Oblivion taking over the world and stuff. You know, who gets which land."

"What?" Elf Guy cocked his head. "You're getting a share of land, too?" I wasn't really sure what I wanted to do.

Just keep stalling, I thought.

"Of course I'm getting a share!" I yelled. "Oblivion is giving me land because I… uh… gave him a box of cookies! Yeah!"

"What?"

"Too bad you're not special enough."

"What?"

"You're just a worthless little lump!"

"What?"

"You haven't done anything to help Oblivion!" I felt the abyssal darkness around me clear away. Elf Guy started to get shrouded in mist. "Useless! Worthless!"

"No, no, no, no." Suddenly, he shot me a glance with his eyes. I was immediately covered in void again. "You have no idea what you are talking about! Wait…" He frowned. "Wasn't I trying to destroy this place?"

"Um…" I glanced around at my friends who were standing next to me, appalled. "No. Remember-"

"Oh, shut up! You're just trying to trick me! Back off!" This time, I did stumble over yet another plant and face-planted (pun not intended) on the ground. Luckily, Sarah was there to pick me back off the ground.

"Aha!" Elf Guy cried. "Here we are!" We stepped out onto the roof of the building. I surveyed the area. There wasn't much, just a gravel floor and a few air vents lying around. "Now you have nowhere to run, cowards!"

"Then let's fight!"

"Nah. Fighting isn't my type. I just prefer to talk and talk until my opponent is weakened. Then, bam with the spear. It's awesome."

"Okay." I racked my brain for any possible way out of this situation but came up with no ideas.

"Then bring it on!" Sarah squeaked. She was a whole lot braver than me, even if she sounded afraid right now. "What could go wrong?"

The answer was, unfortunately, a lot of things.

"Gah! I'll deal with you quickly and conquer the building! Starting with you, pretty blond girl! Hmm…" He scratched his spotless chin. "Ah. I see. You tried to defend your mother from certain death."

"You dare-"

"And you failed. Too bad, poor girl. Obviously too weak to even do such a simple task."

"Like you could do any better," I muttered. He didn't hear me.

"You, blond boy! You, along with the pretty blond girl were off fighting-" His voice drowned out from my head.

How dare he insult my friends like that. I felt all my rage gather up in my throat, ready to explode at any second.

"And you!" he boomed. "The elemental. Totally useless- Hey! Why aren't you getting mad?"

"Stupid," I grumbled under my breath. "Disgracing my friends… hurting them."

"Get mad, elemental! Why aren't my powers working anymore?"

Dust and ash swirled around my legs, creating a shield of impenetrable debris.

"Whatever. I'll just charge!" He quickly struck down my shocked friends who were just standing there, aghast and pale, and turned to me.

Just as he faced me, all the emotions that had been building up in my throat: malice and wrath for my enemies, anguish for the fallen ones, but most of all love for all my friends and family, all exploded out of me in one blast.

Chapter 12

This time, my dream was kind of funny and also kind of frightening.

Oblivion, now as Selena was resting in a rocking chair in his camp, which was half repaired from the time we had demolished it.

"Why did I take this body?" he growled. "I hate-"

"Pigs! Monkeys! Punch me!" he suddenly squealed. He punched himself.

"Shut up, stupid girl!" The stupid girl shut up.

I wanted to see more of Oblivion acting like a fool, but my dream violently cracked and shattered.

...

Elf Guy was gone. Most of the building was gone. My stomach seemed to have gone on vacation with Signus to play poker at Las Vegas.

Yohan and Sarah were sitting near me in one of the not-destroyed classrooms. Once they saw that I was awake, they grinned and turned to talk to me.

"That was awesome," Yohan said. His face brandished a long slash across his cheek. "You just unleashed a blast of pure energy at that guy, and he instantly vaporized."

"Let him rest a bit," Sarah interrupted, putting her hand on his shoulder. "Go to sleep, Will. By the way, you still haven't taken a shower." I nodded groggily and closed my eyes once again. Somehow, something was missing next to me.

Then I remembered. Selena used to always sleep next to me like a good old faithful puppy dog.

Now, where was she? I sighed and tried to squeeze tears out of my eyes.

"Are you missing her?" Sarah asked. So much for letting me rest. "Are you missing Selena?" Next to her, Yohan grumbled something about Sarah being a hypocrite and stomped away.

"Yes. Very."

"Don't worry. We all miss her. But she'll stay strong, even with Oblivion inside her body." She patted my back for reassurance.

"You'll be fine. Don't worry. Don't cry." Wow, she really sounded like my mother whenever I got hurt.

"Thanks. I feel better now."

"Okay. Good. Rest now, take a nap. I'll wake you in the morning." I nodded and went to sleep.

In the morning, Sarah lightly shook me, and I got up, stretching.

"Big day today, eh?" she said. "It's the twenty-eighth, about nine o'clock. We are about to head over to Alumenta's place, but we don't know where it is."

"Oh, that's easy. Selena said something about having to be stupid enough to get to her castle."

"Then Yohan would qualify."

"Hey!"

"So maybe…" I thought for a moment. "If we just jump from this building here, we might end up in his castle."

"And if we don't?"

"We go splat on the ground."

"That's cheerful. Well, we better hurry. Time's running out."

We headed to the highest point of the edifice and jumped off. The wind whipped in our faces, and just as we were about to get crushed into the earth like pancakes, the ground opened up and swallowed us.

…

We ended up on a cold stone floor, not able to see anything. It was pitch black.

"Hello?" I called. "Anybody?"

"Hey!" Sarah's voice suddenly complained. "That's my face, Yohan, not a brick."

"Your brain is like a brick."

"Look who's talking."

Yohan summoned a fireball, casting an aura of light around the surrounding area. I quickly got up and hurried next to my friends.

"Why is it dark?" I asked.

"We need to find out, I guess."

We strolled around through hallways and looked into rooms. Not finding anything, I sat down, discouraged.

"Maybe, instead of finding trouble, we'll let trouble find us," Sarah said. "That's always worked out, huh?"

And it did work out. (Kind of.)

We heard some clamor coming from the right side of the hallway that we were in. *Thump, thump, thump.*

"Get ready," Yohan whispered. "For whatever's coming."

In a great flash of light, a colossal figure, cloaked in a mantle drawn over with runes descended onto the floor. She snapped her fingers, and torches blazed in the walls.

"Well, then my dears." Her face was so disorienting that I couldn't stare at it for longer than a second, and her hair was multicolored and constantly changing. "Have you come to bow down to Oblivion and help his cause?"

"Uh…"

"Perfect!" she exclaimed. "We definitely need new recruits sooner or later. Let's take you to the initiation-"

"Wait!" Sarah cried. "You're working for Oblivion now?"

197

"Duh! Oblivion is going to rule the world with me in second command. It will be amazing!"

"Oblivion's going to destroy the world, not conquer the world. If he wins, then there won't be any world to rule."

"Oh, sure. Those commercials on television are just trying to fool you."

"There are commercials on television?" I said. "Actually, never mind. So you've been giving monsters super speed?"

"And super strength," she added. "I'm planning to also add super regeneration to the package, too."

"So, are you one of those goddesses that gets stronger once the bad guys get stronger?" I ventured.

"That? Sure I am. I used to be on Oblivion's side, but then I switched back to Reality's side. But now I'm back to Oblivion's side because Reality is going to lose."

"How'd you know?"

"I used a foresight rune. Bad things are coming for Reality and his people. If you are on his side, just come to us. We will rule the world together!"

"I'd rather not," Sarah muttered under her breath.

"Hey, where's that Selena girl? She was good at using runes."

"Selena is… possessed by Oblivion right now," I said quietly. "How about we don't talk about that?"

"She is?" Alumenta sounded genuinely surprised. "Well that's why Oblivion looked so pretty all of a sudden. That other guy? Ew. Dyed hair. Definitely not my taste." I wanted to mention that she herself had dyed hair, but I decided not to say anything.

"So, would you kindly disable these runes that you put on the monsters, please? Right now would be great." Sarah managed a fake smile.

"Hmm, that's a good question." She tapped on her chin. "No."

"Please. Oblivion… uh… ordered us to do so."

"Nah. I met with him a few hours ago, and he didn't mention anything about that. And the only way to disable the runes is to disable me. And even a disability would only last a day or so. But you're just talking junk, wasting my time. Go into one of my cells, would you?" She waved her hand, and we were teleported into another stone brick room with bars facing outward onto a dark hallway.

"That went great," I mumbled. "At least we have time to plan now."

"She's really weird," Yohan mentioned.

"She seemed so much different than when I met her before. She was all serious last time."

"She is getting more powerful with Oblivion getting more powerful. That's probably what's making her talk all weird. The same thing happened with Abyssion, right?"

"Yeah," I agreed. "So, we need to disable her somehow. Does she literally mean "disable"? Like break her legs?"

"Maybe. If so, that'll be easy," Yohan said.

"Easier said than done," Sarah warned. "We need a better plan than that."

"We could try to deflect a rune back at her," I said. "And knock out her legs, right?"

"Last time we did that…"

"Okay. Let's not try that then."

"Wait!" She held up a finger. "I have another idea, very risky…" Her voice died down as she leaned in to tell us her plan.

…

"Okay," I said after she finished. "That sounds not plausible. But we don't have any other ideas. I guess we have to go for it."

"One problem at a time, though. How do we get out?" Yohan scratched his head and shook the bars. "They're probably charmed with some kind of rune."

"Let's just blast them open!"

"Alumenta probably did something to

prevent that to happen, just saying."

"So, have you decided yet?" Alumenta suddenly appeared in front of us, and the prison bars broke open. "Are you going to join Oblivion's side-the winning side, or Reality's losing side? By the way, if you choose Reality, you won't leave this place alive!"

"We choose Reality!" I shouted, raising Malachite. "Now fight us!"

"What? Oh, no, dears. You won't be fighting-" An arrow whistled past her ear. "You won't be fighting me! I'll just-"

We started barraging her with our powers, and she sighed. "I guess I just have to take you out myself." She drew out a staff and rapidly fired runes around the room.

"Over here, you idiot!" Sarah called, waving her hands wildly. "Can you even see?" I ducked behind Alumenta and tried for a slash under her cloak.

No chance. She whipped around and shot a levitation rune at me, and up I went into the ceiling.

"You know what really annoys me?" she said.

"What?"

"The gods are so full of themselves, they don't even know who to call minor gods and goddesses. You know Alluvion? He is among the most powerful gods, yet they still call him minor.

Oblivion is smart enough to realize that, though, and that is why he sent Solaria to assault his castle."

"So?" Her staff made contact with my leg, and I went crashing into a wall. "OW!"

"See? Me, a minor goddess, just defeated you!" Ropes snapped around my arms, and I was pinned to the ground.

Soon, Alumenta had both Sarah and Yohan tied up and tossed next to me. She tapped on her chin. "Now what do we do with you three? Toss you into a pit full of traps?"

"Sure," Sarah said. "Just please don't-"

"Maybe have you swim in a pool of lava?"

"Okay, but-"

"Don't do what?" she demanded. "Will this be the best way to torture you?"

"Yes. You can do all of those things, but don't use an acid rune. Please." Her voice was pretty convincing.

This was our plan. I remembered one of the fairy tales my mom used to read to me. It was called Briar Rabbit and the Tar Baby, where a fox tried to catch Briar Rabbit with a sticky figurine made out of tar.

He managed to trap the rabbit but was tricked because of what the rabbit had said.

Torture me all you want, my mom read. *Just don't throw me into the briar bush.* Then the fox threw him into the briar bush, letting him escape accidentally.

Let's just hope that Alumenta didn't read fairy tales.

"Hmm. Are you tricking me? Or are you not?" Sarah was actually crying now (probably fake crying, who knows). "Just don't use the acid rune! Please!"

"Okay, okay. I'll use the acid rune!" She launched a rune with a nauseous shade of lime at us. It exploded into deadly fumes, and we closed our mouths and eyes to avoid the poison. It still stung a little, but it wasn't overwhelming.

"Now!" Yohan cried. All of us, at the same time, fired flaming projectiles into the acid.

With a loud *Boom!*, all the acid and fire combusted and exploded into a raging inferno.

"Ahh!" Alumenta screamed. "My eyes! I can't see!" We crawled out from the flames and cut the bindings off of ourselves.

"Now what?" I asked. "Did that do it?" *Whoosh!* A strong wind blew the fire down the hallway.

"I will hunt you down with your fire!" Alumenta screeched. "I-" I didn't listen to what she said. We ran.

...

I had no idea where we were headed. I just

knew that we had to get as far away from the fire as we could.

Soon, we stumbled into a barracks full of Oblivion monsters. I yelled, "Run! There's a fire!" Most believed us. Some decided to stay because they were playing a very intense match of cards.

Alarms started blaring in the castle. We burst out into another hallway, dodging flying runes and arrows.

"Get them! Get them!" Alumenta's voice shrieked. I hoped that the monsters didn't know who to catch and ended up capturing Alumenta herself.

"Where do we go?" Sarah gasped. "There's nowhere to go!" We looked left and right. We could either choose diving straight into a poisonous fire or into some bloodthirsty Oblivion warriors.

"Go to the Oblivion monsters! We won't survive in the fire," Yohan said.

"Even you?"

"It's acid, Will! How do we survive acid?"

"I hoped-"

"No talking!" Sarah snapped. "Let's just get out of here!" We shot straight into the monsters, occasionally slicing and avoiding attacks.

Just as we were about to get overwhelmed, a tremor rumbled through the castle and caused the Oblivion soldiers to collapse.

"The castle is losing its grip on Reality!"

Sarah said. "We have to get out now!"

"How do you know?"

"Hey! Just because I'm blonde doesn't mean that I'm stupid, Will! This thing is falling into the Endless Abyss right now."

"So what do we do?"

"Run!"

"Run where?"

"Well, that's a good question. We could try jumping again," she suggested.

"Into the void? No way! And-"

"The fire's coming near! Let's move!" We sprinted away again, not really sure where to go.

"How did you exit this place last time?" Yohan panted. "It would great if we could do the same thing!" Another vibration threw us all sideways into the wall.

"Alumenta dropped us into Yharon's jungle! I don't think she'll do that this time!"

"Or maybe we can!" Sarah said.

"You are crazy." Yohan shook his head. "She's never going to do that. She might drop us into the Endless Abyss, but what good would that be?"

"We could reason with her. C'mon. Follow the trail of runes. That'll lead us there." She took his hand, and we now went in search of Alumenta.

The trail of runes (that should have led us straight to Alumenta) leading to nowhere were very useless and confusing. Then, we were chased by the fire from multiple directions until we were trapped.

"Well," I sighed. "It's been nice knowing you guys."

"Quiet, you! We can find a way out of here!" Sarah snapped.

"We can make the flames die down. Help us, Will." I nodded and focused on the roaring blaze.

Water. The ocean. Put the fire out. Suddenly, a wall of water rushed through the hall like a flash flood and doused the conflagration down to nothing.

Unfortunately, we were also soaking wet.

"You have to be kidding, Will," Sarah groaned.

"At least I put out the fire, right? And I took a shower, just like you wanted."

"This is salt water!"

"Hey, I'm sorry."

"Aha!" Alumenta screeched. "I put the fire out!"

"That was me," I muttered.

"And I caught the runaways!" She pointed a finger straight at us and beckoned for us to come closer. "Cuties, you have managed to defeat me because you wrecked my palace, but that doesn't mean that you'll escape. I promised, remember?"

"Look, Alumenta. Oblivion is going to reduce the world to nothing. He's already in the process of doing it. We are falling into part of his

206

domain right now. Do you want to live in a world like this? Nothing but darkness?"

"Oh but there is a world down there," she said, smiling coldly. "It's where all the cursed souls go. And you, blond girl, shall find your mother down there." She waved her hand, and we were in Oblivion's territory, on a tall hill at the bottom of the Endless Abyss.

Man, this place was even worse than Elf Guy's eyes.

Everywhere was faded purple and ebony, with gnarled burnt trees sticking out of the ground like spikes. As far as the eye could see, there were drifting spirits, some pulsing a malevolent shade of crimson while others were glowing dim blue.

"Oh, jeez," I mumbled. "How the heck do we get out of this place now?" Then I realized that Sarah was bowed down before a ghost: the ghost of her mother.

"Why are you down here?" Sarah cried. "You don't deserve to be down here. You should have a happy afterlife, not this!"

"Dear, I am down here because I died thinking that my daughter would be eternally grieved by me."

"But that's not fair!" she protested.

"Some things are not fair, Sarah. Stay strong. Today will be the final day, whether you succeed against Oblivion."

"But if we defeat him, will this place be destroyed too? Will I never be able to see you again?"

"That I do not know." She put her ghostly hand on Sarah and kissed her forehead. "I love you, Sarah." The breeze picked up and blew the specter away into a million particles.

Yohan was the first to interject into the silence. "That was depressing. Well, at least we know that today's going to be the final day. We better enjoy it."

"Okay." Sarah got back off the ground and linked arms with Yohan. "We first have to get out of this place. Any ideas?"

"None," I answered. "How about we take a walk around and get our brain cells flowing, shall we?"

As we took a hike through the dreary landscape of the Endless Abyss, I let my thoughts roam free.

We have to defeat Oblivion. But how did we manage to defeat any of the other baddies? Selena took down Abaddon. But she took down Abaddon with her anger. I overcame Elf Guy by releasing all of my emotions. Solaria… not so much.

But I have to conquer Oblivion with happiness.

"Hey. Earth to Will." Yohan was tapping on my head with his knuckles. "Could you, by any chance, teleport us out of this place, because we have a problem."

"What's new?"

"Nothing. But there's a huge a parade of spirits headed in our direction, and they do not look friendly."

"What?" I looked up. "Holy smokes." Spread across the blackened ground was an entire army of blood-red ghosts, shaking violently and sputtering.

"Try a teleport rune."

I tried and ended up shooting a violet firework into the air, signaling all nearby monsters to come and eat our faces.

"That didn't work," I said.

"Surprising. And oh my…" Sarah pointed at the foggy sky, and we watched in terror as Alumenta's castle, on fire and falling apart in several areas, descended rapidly to crush us and the phantom army.

"Hide!" We frantically searched for a shelter alcove and found nothing but a very crooked tree. It was better than nothing as the mighty palace crushed the hiding spot, nearly turning us into human hamburgers.

"We survived!" I squeaked.

"Not so fast!" Alumenta was back again.

"Will you ever be able to get away from us?"

"No! It's time for you to get captured again, cuties!" She shot a rune at us, a rune that would bind us with ropes, but I deflected it with Malachite. It came flying right back at her.

Bindings wrapped around her arms and legs, pinning her down and leaving her powerless.

"We'll be back, Alumenta," I said. "And hopefully you'll decide to choose the right side this time."

"Hey! No! Wait!"

"Think about going back to Sequoia," I whispered. "We have to teleport back there." All of us closed our eyes and concentrated.

Nothing happened.

"Ha! You can't teleport out of here! But I can! Just release me-" A dim pale glow shone from us.

"Goodbye, Alumenta. We'll see you in a bit."

Chapter 13

We landed on the top of the massive tree. Now what?

Two Grovites had to make a ladder out of vines and tree roots to help us get to the ground. One thanked us for being here and told, "New reinforcements have arrived for the enemy, and they're charging into battle right now. You should go check it out."

We rushed up the dirt path to the intersection between Moro Rock and the road up to the top of the mountain, where the battle was being fought.

The reinforcements were Scorpio and his scorpion army.

I had fought Scorpio a year ago when we were on our quest to get the Key of Nightmares from Abaddon. An old guy called Aggergard wanted us to get a scorpion from Scorpio's headquarters in Florida.

Now he was back again, ready to shred our army. His pincers were glistening and tipped with green liquid and his shell like an impenetrable bulwark.

The fight was not going well. Scorpio and his army stood from a distance firing thick dark stingers that pierced through the Grovite shield wall and sent them into a frenzy. At this rate, we would be defeated in about two seconds.

"Coward!" I shouted. "Come and fight! Don't stay back like that! Or are you not brave?" Behind me, Kam murmured, "He sounds like a duck who got run over with a car."

A ripple of uneasiness spread through the crowd. Was Scorpio a good leader?

"YEAH! Come and fight!"

"Ignore him!" the giant scorpion growled. "He's just talking nonsense!"

"But are you a brave leader?" one of the monsters asked.

"Silence! You dare challenge me, little runt?" He turned and glared at his army with his black beady eyes.

"N-no, sir. Sorry sir."

"Good. Cease fire and charge!"

Now I regretted telling Scorpio to charge, because having mutant insects barrel right at you is not as fun as it sounds.

"Oh, gosh." Sarah's teeth started chattering. "No bugs, please. No way." She leaned onto Yohan's shoulder.

"Scaredy-cat!" Kam taunted. "Scared of bugs!"

"Hey!" Rowen said next to her. "Don't be mean. I'm scared of bugs too. And heights. And-"

"Whatever." she rolled her eyes. "I seem to be the least afraid person here, I guess." Now Kam was really getting on my nerves. "What have you done? Why don't you just shut your mouth up for once and help?" That seemed to daunt Kam a bit, but she shrugged and flashed away with her Swiss Army knife.

"It's fine," I told Sarah. "You can stay back."

"I have to go-" Yohan put a hand on her shoulder. "Look. We'll be fine. You can stay back this time." She nodded.

I faced the monstrous Scorpio and pointed at him. "I'll battle you now."

Instantly, he lunged right on top of me, but I ducked and slid under his body. I quickly got off the ground and faced him again with Malachite raised.

"I defeated you before." My voice quivered. "I'll just defeat you again, now."

"But you didn't defeat me at all. I wasn't even close to being defeated. But your stupid friends came in and ruined our party. This time, you don't have any friends."

"Or maybe I do! They're just busy right now."

"Ha!" A tinger whizzed past my ear, and he pounced again. This time, I wasn't so lucky and was buried under a mass of poisonous scorpion and shell. Continuously stabbing upward with Malachite, I rolled away from Scorpio and jumped on top of him.

"Get off!" He whipped around, trying to get

me off while I attempted in vain to crack his carapace.

Realizing too late, we arrived at the edge of the cliff and spiraled off the side.

"Will!" Sarah cried.

"I'll be fine! Don't worry!" I thought she winked at me, but then she was gone. We landed with a harsh thump on a steep slope, Scorpio still beneath me. I hoped that he would have been injured by the fall, he wasn't even near hurt, so I would have to think of a better way to defeat him.

Down the rocky terrain we went, tumbling over each other, colliding into piles of rocks and trees, and scratching against the rough surface of the earth.

Oh gosh, I thought. A lake was approaching rapidly. I launched myself off the monster and landed hard inside a thorny bush. One of the spikes had cleaved a long mark down my leg.

"I've got you!" Scorpio bellowed triumphantly. He lumbered casually to my spot in the brambles. "The demigod can't run anymore, huh?"

"You- you haven't caught me yet." I tried to crawl away. My head throbbed. He poked at me with one of his pincers.

"I could just use my tail on you right now, but you deserve a more painful death after causing so much destruction and interfering with my plans.

Maybe poison…" He tapped his chin thoughtfully.

"My friends will stop you." I backed up into another bush. "You will fail." Something rustled in the tree behind Scorpio.

"Where are your friends, hmm? I don't see them."

"They will save me."

"Oh, little elemental. He needs saving from his friends? That's surprising. I always thought that you were the one flying around, saving people."

"I am," I responded. "But you also need support from other friends. That's why you'll fail, Scorpio. Even when I'm hurt and bleeding, we still will defeat you. I have a helper. You are alone."

"What helper?" He looked around suspiciously, inspecting every hiding spot with his tiny dark eyes.

"She's here. You just can't find her."

"There's nobody!" he declared. "Well, then. It's time to-" Right before he could step forward and slam me on the head with his arm, Sarah Miller dropped out of a tree and landed on Scorpio's head.

For a moment, I was as taken aback as Scorpio. He thrashed and reared, but Sarah was like a leech sticking onto his head.

"Get off!"

"Ahh, this is scary! Run, Will!" Sarah's reminder jarred me back to reality, and I took off into the woods.

Will Sarah be okay? My mind wondered. *Oh no. She hates bugs. What if- No. I won't think about that.* I finally settled next to a massive Sequoia, waiting for my friend.

A few minutes later, Sarah burst into my hiding spot. She looked terrible. Long slashes ran down her pale, white face and covered her jeans. One of her eyes was swollen and purple, and she was limping on her left foot.

"Need- healing," she gasped and crumpled into my arms. I chanted the healing spell over and over again until her face restored to its normal color and her wounds closed up.

"What happened there?"

"I saw you fall off the cliff. I followed you using a rope to climb down the mountain and hid in a bush ready to ambush Scorpio. But please, I hate bugs so much, I don't know how to face him again." She leaned against the tree, steading her breath.

"You were great back there. You faced him even though you were afraid of him. I couldn't ask for you to be any braver than that. Thank you." Somewhere from the forest, the scorpion roared in rage.

"We need to go." She gripped my hand as Scorpio appeared in the clearing. "Run!"

Even with her broken foot and her various lesions, she could sprint fast when she needed to. We flew through the rough vegetation and were just about to reach the mountain again when our enemy landed down right in front of us.

"Morning. Nice day, isn't it?" He grinned. (Can scorpions grin?) "Just like you said, demigod, you need friends to help you. Guess what?"

I answered for him. "You brought friends."

Five giant scorpions surrounded us completely, effectively trapping us in our position. They all fired their stingers at once, and I summoned up the earth to block the shots.

It had been awhile since I had used the earth as my weapon; in fact, it was all the way back in Yharon's castle when we were trying to rescue Vesuvius when I used the element.

"We've trapped you," he snarled. "Now lay down your weapons and surrender.

"Emotions!" I suddenly gasped. "We can use emotions!" I remembered when I was thinking back in the Endless Abyss about how we defeated some of our enemies with emotions.

Abaddon was anger. Yharon was fear. Elf Guy was all of my emotions. Oblivion hopefully would be happiness. Now I would just have to find the right emotion for Scorpio.

"What are you talking about?" he barked. "Emotions? You have no idea what you are thinking."

"What do you mean?" I hollered back. "You have no idea what you're thinking! Your head is totally empty-"

"That's not working," Sarah said.

"Okay. We're going to have to test which emotion is linked to him. This might take a couple tries, but we'll get it someday."

"We don't have days. We have a few seconds. C'mon, Will! Think!"

"So lay down your weapons!" Scorpio hissed. "Hurry up!"

"Okay, Scorpio! We'll do that gladly!" The scorpion didn't say anything.

"This isn't working either," Sarah reminded. "So let's not lay our weapons down."

Scorpio lashed out and knocked Sarah. He held her throat right next to his pincer.

"Do you want me to repeat what I said? Lay down your weapons, or this girl is dead."

I didn't know what to do while I just stood there, helpless. Sarah shook her head and told me to keep on the fight while my mind wanted me to just surrender to the enemy.

But I had to save Sarah. I was not losing another one of my friends. Slowly, I set Malachite down on the ground and fiercely jerked my hands up. Spikes of rock drove up out of the ground, impaling the smaller scorpions and knocking Scorpio off balance.

"Let's go!" I called. We rushed around the side of the mountain, Scorpio trailing behind us.

Soon, we were trapped between a towering mountain and a steep drop down into a lake.

"We're trapped. We could either climb-" She shook her head to herself. "No way. We have to jump into the water, Will."

"What? But-"

"I know how much you hate water. You might even hate water more than me. But we have to face your fear about water just as I'm facing my fear of bugs."

"I've caught you now!" Scorpio cackled.

"He's said that multiple times already, and we've escaped," I muttered. "But as much as I hate water, you're right. I have to jump." We leaped over the edge.

"Noooo!" Stingers whizzed by and splashed into the water. "Get back!" As we fell, rain started pouring along with a heavy wind.

Aquaia, I prayed. *Please save us. I know I've been rude and-*

We hit the water.

The cold was so shocking that I could have just sunk to the bottom of the water and not noticed. Sarah tugged on my sleeve and reminded me to float back up to the surface.

First, there was just one little problem: I didn't really know how to swim well.

I ended up doggy-paddling through the freezing water through kelp and fish to the fresh air.

Gagging and coughing, we flung ourselves against the dirt that was releasing an earthy aroma because of the rain.

"That," I said. "Was absolutely terrible."

"You made it, Will." Sarah looked in better condition than me, even with her injuries and her being related to fire. "We escaped him."

FOOM! A giant scorpion plummeted from the air and landed with a splash in the water.

"You have to be kidding me!" I was about to scream in frustration. "Next time Sarah, please knock on some wood." She nodded. "That will do. If we survive this time."

"I seriously don't want to run any longer." I sat down on a rock and sighed.

Will!"

"Sorry." And then I did scream in frustration, just as Scorpio crawled out of the water.

A wave of red light rippled out of me, hitting trees and bushes and instantly decaying them. The water instantly turned gray and corroded, just like the Corruption.

Scorpio looked up, aghast as the wave of crimson swept over him and turned him into dust.

"Well, then, that works too," Sarah said. "Nice job." There was no *Oh my gosh, Will! You just defeated my mortal enemy! Thanks so much!* Just *Nice job.* I groaned and put my head in my hands. Never before had I been so discouraged in my life, and I didn't even know why I was.

"Will, we have another problem right now, okay? We have to get out of this place."

"Can't you use your rope?" I mumbled. "That would be easy."

"I can't. Maybe use your earth powers and get us out of here." So I just had to use my powers to propel us out of there and back to the main battle.

Up at the mountain, Yohan was waiting for us and tapping his foot. His hair had grown longer and he hadn't cut it yet, so he was tying it into a messy ponytail.

"Mornin'," he said. "Nice weather, isn't it?"

"Great weather," Sarah agreed. "Now what are you doing to your hair? Here, let me make you a good ponytail." He shrugged and let Sarah proceed into making his hair into an enormous misshapen bun. She winked at me, and I decided not to say anything about it.

"So, did you defeat Scorpio?"

"Yeah. It was very frustrating. What happened up here?" He traced his hand down the scrape on his face.

"We were fighting. Then a breeze came through and all the scorpions just dispersed back into the mountain. I assumed that you had defeated him, so I came here to wait."

"Is there a new round of monsters coming soon?" Sarah asked. "We should get ready."

"More monsters should be coming soon... Hey! What'd you do to my hair?" Sarah broke down laughing, and even I cracked a small grin after being so down.

"Good job doing my hair, Miss. Annoying."

"You're welcome Mr. Yo-Yo."

"Hey!" he protested. "Nina was the one who came up with that name. Let's not use it."

"Sure, buddy." Sarah returned his hair to ponytail form. "When is-" A row of flaming red arrows shot over our heads.

"Ready to fight?" Yohan said.

"No."

"That's great. Now let's go."

I was sick and tired of battling against monsters. Couldn't they give a break? I wanted an intermission in the war, just long enough for me to rush to a beach with my friends and slouch there the whole day.

And it was just my luck too, Oblivion was leading the approach to the tree wearing just Selena's regular outfit: a white Fort Azari shirt with jeans but also with a dark cloak, occasionally squeaking "Cow!" or "Food!". The random words coming out of his mouth were a nuisance but not too interfering.

With one swipe of his weapon, which was, unfortunately Vesuvius (all that hard work getting that staff back, and there it was in his hand), he brought down a dozen warriors.

"He's unstoppable," I whispered. "There's no way." Now Oblivion was imbued with Selena's agile movement and deadly sword-wielding skills.

"Hey! Don't feel down. We'll figure out a way to beat him some way." Sarah patted my back.

I began slicing monsters to dust, unleashing a blast of energy if I was swarmed by too many enemies, and ducking to avoid the occassional arrow that flew by.

Soon the monsters stampeded over our broken army and surged toward the giant tree. We formed a protective ring around it while Grovite enchanters held up a green forcefield around the tree. Sometimes, a lance or projectile would fly over our heads and collide into the shield, causing one Grovite to collapse from exhaustion.

"Onward!" Oblivion cried. "Moo! Donkey!" There had to be a way to escape this ring of a handful of defenders surrounded by a sea of monsters. But the more I thought about it, the more annoyed I got. Why wasn't this battle fair? Shouldn't we get more soldiers too?

I screamed in frustration and blasted all the surrounding adversaries back into the waiting spear points of the monsters behind them.

"Again, that works too," Sarah remarked. "Wow." The shout left my ears ringing and in pain, and I was sure that all the attackers experienced the same thing except magnified one hundred times.

I took the chance and ran up to Oblivion to strike him down while his ears were still stinging. Right as I was going to give him a nice stab in the chest, I paused.

This wasn't Oblivion's body, was it? It was Selena's body. I couldn't stab Selena.

Unfortunately, while I was in deep thought, Oblivion came to his senses and punched me with Selena's fist so hard that I flew back and shattered the forcefield around the tree completely. Man, Selena had some muscle.

"NO!" Everyone was helpless and couldn't do anything as Oblivion raised Vesuvius and cut straight through the tree.

"YES!" he cackled. "The sky defeats the Earth. Now even Reality's own forces will be at war with each other!"

I thought it was over. Oblivion had defeated Earth. Now what? Would it start cracking and split apart?

There was an awkward silence as nothing happened. We all stared at the Oblivion-Selena with Vesuvius raised in the air.

"You didn't win yet," I squeaked.

"Of course not!" he bellowed. "I am off to elsewhere to- moo!- actually defeat this universe. I will destroy the core of the gods and goddesses- oink!- while you wait here helpless. My army will guard you for now."

And of course, we didn't listen and sprang into action. The tree toppled and crushed a row of giants. It released ripples and ripples of fresh energy that smelled like the best parts of nature which rejuvenated the tired (everyone) and healed the wounded (everyone).

During the chaos, Oblivion slipped away back up the winding path to elsewhere.

"Follow him!" I yelled while jumping over piles of burning tree bark and dust clouds made of the remains of monsters. Now that was a smell that I never wanted to get a whiff of again. Sarah and Yohan nodded and sprinted after me.

Oblivion weaved his way through the thick shrubbery, trying to lose us by taking an alternate route.

"I know where he's going," Sarah said. "He's going up to that mountain we went to."

"How do you know?"

"I just know. This is it. It's where either he's going to win or we're going to win."

"But-"

"No buts! I just feel it in my bones. Let's take the easy route up there and hopefully beat him to the top."

I wanted to argue, but the situation was finally sinking in. This was it. This was where it would be the destruction of everything on Earth, or the defeat of Oblivion. For the past few days, I was dreading the moment, but it was finally happening. We were going to face Oblivion, alone, without any reinforcements at hand.

And secretly, I also knew that a few hours from now, I would know if Selena survived this ordeal. If Earth just got obliterated, nobody would be left anyway, so it didn't matter. But if we won and Selena didn't make it through, I… how about we not think about it.

I decided to think on the bright side and ignore the nag in my mind that David didn't survive his experience with Oblivion.

"Here we are." Through all of my thinking, I hadn't realized that we had marched all the way up to the peak of Sequoia without me even realizing. The surroundings were still as beautiful as ever but had a sinister glare about them.

With a shock, I saw that the sky was actually red, as if Cataclysm had taken over it. Knowing my luck, Cataclysm probably had taken over the dark, clouded sky and was preparing to launch an astral comet at my face to blow me to smithereens.

"This is nerve-racking," Yohan muttered, breaking the silence. "Very nerve-racking." We hiked over to the center of the plateau next to the rock where my two friends had sat, chatting. I did not feel like chatting today.

Oblivion broke out onto the clearing,

muttering to himself about how all the branches were so itchy when he spotted us. His face broke into an evil sneer, which did not look pretty on Selena's face.

"So you've come to stop me?" He slowly strolled forward toward us, every step echoing throughout the mountain like a cannon blast. "I don't think so."

Now Earth started trembling. Fractures formed in the ground, and magma pooled out in the divots of the dirt beneath us.

"Stand back," I said, my voice shaking just like my knees. "We will stop you."

"How?" His laughter was just like Elf Guy's laughter, rolling in waves of doom over us. "I know you have already experienced- honk!- the pain of Aggergard."

"Wait, who? Elf Guy is Aggergard?"

"You didn't know, foolish child? Well of course you didn't know. I redeemed him from his position, gave him another chance. He will be the one destroying Abaddon and Signus, of course. You see, gods and goddesses are cruel. It may seem that we are the ones who punish and torture, but it really isn't the case. Gods are no better than us, you hear that?"

"Less talk, more fighting!" I demanded. "Or are you too scared to fight three puny demigods?"

"Sure, I will." He looked at Yohan and Sarah,

who were sagging from the rain pounding on their heads. "Actually, I think I'm fighting two and a half demigods. It appears that these friends of yours aren't faring very well. How about a little wake-up call?" He raised Vesuvius into the air and smashed a meteor into the boulder behind him, spattering them with earthen shrapnel.

"All awake? Then let's fight."

I charged Oblivion with Malachite raised in my hand. Unfortunately, Malachite was going to be as useful as a lump of rocks now, since the tree had fallen. Instead, an elemental dagger was going to be my weapon of choice that I would battle with.

"Your friend's body not faring too well, eh?" He swung the staff as I ducked and narrowly dodged the attack, hoping to sneak in for a hit.

The good news: I hit him. The bad news: it was not effective and just bounced off his armor like it was a rubber ball.

With his next swing, I somehow caught Vesuvius on my blade and thrust it upwards.

"Don't hurt her."

"Oh, don't worry. She's in plenty of pain right now, but in a few minutes, I won't need a mortal body anymore. I've been gathering power, so I'll use my energy to form my own body."

"So what will happen?" I asked. Vesuvius knocked the dagger out of my hand, and it clattered to the ground. The staff then caught me square in the chest and sent me face-first into the ground. Oblivion picked the knife up and sliced it down my back, leaving a long streak.

"Your friend's body will dissolve. She will forever be conscious in excruciating pain, wondering why her friend ever sent me into her soul."

"Will!" Sarah cried, rushing over to my side. I lifted my face off the ground and looked at Yohan swimming in the lava. Maybe they were recharging. Sarah definitely looked refreshed. Her eyes literally blazed with flames.

"I'm okay," I mumbled. "I think I swallowed an earthworm."

"AWAY!" Oblivion bellowed. He hit Sarah with his staff and blasted her back into the lava swimming pool.

The earth was rippling. Magma was flowing. Raindrops were splashing on the ground. The breeze started whipping up harder and harder.

"All four elements, all together!" he proclaimed. "All together for me to crush them!"

What do I do? I wondered. *Sarah is hurt. I am hurt. The world is ending. Hmm… that's a slight problem too.*

"This- woof! THAT'S ENOUGH!" he roared. Selena's blackened eyes flickered back to their normal sky blue color, and she screamed in pain.

Now I've only heard Selena scream a few times, and they were all because of enjoyment. This time, it wasn't enjoyment. It was pure pain, and it was the worst sound I ever heard.

"Please," I begged. "Stop."

"Happiness," Sarah croaked. Her voice sounded a million miles away. "Think happy thoughts, Will. That is the key." She then went silent, and I hoped that the worst hadn't happened to her.

Happy thoughts. Such a simple thing.

C'mon, Will! I urged. *I can do this.*

As I began my stream of cheerful thoughts, a warm glow started to flow from me, and a magic movie popped up in front of my face.

The first image was one of a bright, sunny day in a grassy field. Sunlight streamed through the tall, vibrant trees that surrounded the clearing. A little toddler with messy black hair, no more than two days old, sat in the lush grass with his mom.

"That's- that's me!" I exclaimed. I was playing peek-a-boo with my mom, laughing and giggling every time my mom revealed her eyes.

"What is this?" Oblivion demanded. "You cannot stop me!" The movie headed onto another scene, this one also of me, now about five or six years old. I was on a seesaw in a colorful kid's playground, going up and down with another little guy.

He was Zach.

Even though the details of his face were unclear, his trademark jeans and shirt were punctuating, along with the fact that he kept toppling off the side of his seat. His clumsiness was obvious; he was just plain old Zach who couldn't morph into different animals.

"Wow, it's Zach," Yohan whispered from behind me. I turned and momentarily lost my focus. Yohan was covered in bruises and slashes, definitely not in good shape for fighting.

"Behold as I reveal my true form!" Oblivion shouted. He spread his arms out, pulsing a deep shade of purple.

"Keep going!" Yohan said. "You can do it!"

The next slide in the film was me just a few months ago. I was situated in my apartment, sitting next to a table while working on my homework with Selena.

"You are very stupid," she muttered. Her voice made a lump in my throat. "You don't even know how to simple algebra, much less geometry."

"I'm sorry, Airhead. I'm not a mathematical genius like you."

"Done with my homework!" she declared. "I'm off to raiding the pantry. Pretty sure there were some cheese puffs in there." The scene faded away and led to another one, this one of me a few years in the future. How I managed to think of that, I'm not sure.

I was sitting on a chair in some breakfast place, holding a coffee cup in one hand and somebody else's hand in the other.

"Cheers." I grinned, clinking cups with whoever I was sitting with. Then the camera angle turned, showing me enjoying some drinks with my friends: Selena, Yohan, Sarah, and Zach.

"Wipe your mouth," Sarah ordered, handing a napkin to Yohan. "You have chocolate all over your face."

Again, the scene changed, this time to something I never saw before. We were in a modern house, sort of like Darkecho's house but with even nicer furniture and an amazing crystal chandelier.

Sarah was playing there with her dad and her mom.

"This is Sarah Miller," I announced, faintly feeling the temperature around me growing higher, the lights shining harder, Oblivion's void weakening. I didn't know where the words were coming from. "She had to deal with her dad, who never paid attention to her. Her mom, the only joy of her life had died, leaving her alone in a huge world. But she found happiness, with her friend, Yohan, and even with the dragon Darkecho who always wanted to eat her." The spirit of Oblivion floated out of Selena's body and fizzled into almost nothing, just a black speck.

"NO! STOP! You can't do this! Please!" Oblivion begged. I didn't want to stop. I couldn't stop. I was losing control.

Keep going, I thought. *This is the final battle.*

"Learn to be happy, to content in whatever you have. Many of my friends have terrible relatives but still are glad with what they have. Selena, one of my best friends, had a dad who ignored her like she was just a pest. She ran away and found a good friend who led her to safety. But then even that friend died, yet she was still content in what she had."

"Quiet-"

"Oblivion. You should have taken another path in your life. Evil always falls under good, no matter how strong evil is. The darkness will not overcome the light."

I was literally light. Oblivion was literally the darkness. The darkness could not overcome the light.

The last thing I saw was black.

Chapter 14

I wasn't the problem here. Even with a slice down my back, various wounds, and a bad hairdo, I was pretty well off (but why did I smell like rotten cottage cheese?).

The worst had happened. Selena was lying on the ground, her face drained of color and masked by her hair that somehow looked like a dirty blonde, not brown, still wearing that hideous (it looked cool and all, but it was Oblivion's so that's why I didn't like it) black cloak. She wasn't breathing at all.

The sun was setting behind the looming mountains in a now clear sky. Would I ever be able to enjoy another sunset with her?

"She's... she's gone," Zach gulped. "I don't think she survived."

"No. She has to be alive. Please Zach." I knelt down beside her and felt her hand. It was clammy and cold.

"I'm sorry Will. So sorry. Even if she was alive, she has some disease in her body eating at her soul." Everyone gathered around her murmured words of appraisal on how valiantly she had fought against Oblivion.

"Something smells," Kam snickered. "Is that you, William?" A few people shot her murderous glances, but I just nodded to shut her up. Apparently satisfied, she walked away spinning her Swiss Army knife around in her hand. I was sure that she would impale herself with that weapon one day.

Just as the sun ducked below the horizon, Selena took a strangled breath and sat straight up. I was so shocked and relieved that I fell back onto my back and just about passed out.

"Hello everyone," she said. "I'm back." She seemed completely healed of any earlier wounds. Her face was back to its normal color, and even her eyes glimmered like a sunny day. Even though she looked just like a normal human being who hadn't been tortured by Oblivion, I knew that she was a master at controlling her emotions and might be traumatized from the experience.

Once she spotted me, she threw herself onto me and hugged me. I made a sound that was sort of like a donkey getting hit by a car and finally smiled.

"What happened? I mean, I'm glad you're back, but did you die? And what about Oblivion being in your body?" She flashed me a look that said *talk about Oblivion later.*

"Well, then." She laughed, quickly releasing me but still holding my arm tight. Hearing her laugh was the best sound ever, but it quickly ended as she turned serious again. "I did die. I was a spirit, floating toward the afterlife. But I couldn't find a way into the place. Then Signus came along and said, "Shoo!", and here I am." She was definitely acting too calm and collected than I would expect. Nobody would just announce that they just came back from the dead because of a past enemy shooing them away.

"Oh thank goodness." Sarah broke down into tears, and we all gathered together for a huge group hug. And that was fun. Instead of just being crushed by one bulldozer, I was squished by the whole construction crew.

"Your medical skills aren't very good, Zachary," Kam said, apparently coming back to watch. "You said she was dead, be she clearly isn't!"

"That's not nice, Kam," Rowen squeaked.

"Whatever! Let's go, boy!" She marched away with Rowen following close behind.

"Let's go somewhere else to talk, alright?" Selena said. "Without all these people." Luckily, most of the demigods had already dispersed, so it was only my friends and me again.

"Into the forest." I pointed at the swaying trees bathed in the moonlight. "And then let's talk."

Everyone nodded in agreement, and we headed into the Sequoia jungle, weaving through vines and roots while Selena told us her story.

"When Oblivion entered my body, it was like a cold wave seeping through my bones, a burning sensation that also felt like I was being frozen. I just knew that I wasn't surviving this. But, just thinking about my friends helped me a lot."

"Well, you didn't survive," I mentioned.

"Please shut up, Will, and let me continue my story. So I was getting that tingling sensation, and then it stopped. I felt just like normal, except that I couldn't see anything and I couldn't control my own movements." She stopped at a shaded area scattered with sittable rocks and plopped on one of them. "Then it felt like I was falling, just falling forever. It felt like there were spikes everywhere, just scraping me and scratching me. It was just like that."

"That sounds fun."

"Please, Will. This is serious."

"No, look." I placed my hand my her shoulder. "I'm sorry. Truly sorry that I put you through this."

"Hey. It's okay. Don't worry."

"But I was the one who put you through all of this. You should be mad at me."

"No." She held her hands up. "I put myself through this. I choose to do this. Don't blame yourself. And also let me continue."

"Sure."

"Sometimes, my vision would flicker, and I would gain control of my body again. That's when I started shouting random stuff like moo and woof, woof."

"He did seem pretty hilarious when he did

that," I admitted.

"Thanks. But I regretted it. Did you hear me scream? He was crushing my soul so hard that I couldn't breathe, couldn't think, couldn't even feel the pain. I felt myself dying, Will, I did."

"You'll be fine," I comforted. "You're here now with us."

But that might not even be the worst part. Ever so often, I would have terrible visions about what Oblivion was thinking. One was just showing the world completely covered in abyss. Another was of us just all confined in dark tiny spaces, with no light and no one to talk to. That one was the worst one. Solitary confinement is cruel. But it was all so real, so alive that I could feel the prison bars on my fingertips." The beginning of tears glistened in her eyes, and I marveled at how she could last so long without just totally breaking down. "Oblivion is cruel. You know, I heard everything he said about gods being terrible and treating mortals with no respect. That's not true. If Oblivion destroyed the world, he would push everyone out of his way. Cataclysm, Aggergard, you name it. Even his own brother. Can you imagine that?"

"No," I answered like a little kindergartener.

"Well, well, well, what do we have here?" Kam broke out onto our secret spot and grinned at us like she had caught us stealing eraser tops from the bin (trust me, I know that expression very well).

"You know what Kam?" Selena snapped. "I'm fed up with you. I don't care what you're trying to do, if you're trying to cut down a tree with that useless knife of yours, just GET OUT!" She pointed a finger back at the foliage she had emerged from.

"Did you just call my knife… useless?" she growled. I was pretty sure that Selena had hit a delicate spot in Kam's mind. She stood up and started bombarding Kam with offense after offense.

"Of course it's useless! The only thing you can cut with that piece of trash is paper, which is only slightly more useful than you! You've done nothing to help our battle! All you've done is blab your mouth off at us while we're hard at work!" The wind started whipping up. "Sorry, Your Highness, but we're not the servants of you." Her cloak was billowing behind her like a black flag." At the least, you should be the servant of me! I have crushed both Abaddon and Yharon-" Kam just turned and fled. "Sorry."

All the wind abruptly stopped, leading to silence.

In all my life listening to Selena yelling at someone, I had never seen such a fierce onslaught of words spilling out of her mouth. I had also never heard her take everything she said back.

"I'm terrible," she moaned, putting her head in her hands. "Oblivion has manipulated my mind to think about the worst of people."

"What? No. It can't be."

"I can just sense the place where people are uncomfortable, and- oh my, I hate this."

"I would rephrase it to Oblivion has trained my mind to think about the worst of people," I suggested. "Because I don't know what manipulated means." From the mass of brown hair came a wave of giggling and snorting that just made me feel ridiculous.

"You are a bit lacking on your vocabulary," Sarah said. "You should go to a tutor."

"Hey, I'm sorry! Most people don't know what Abaddon or Yharon means, right? So I'm smart for my age. Selena is six months older than me! She's fourteen right now! I'm only thirteen!" Suddenly, Selena looked up. "What day is it today, anyway?"

"It's the night of the twenty-eighth. Of December, not Noctomber."

"What is Noctomber?"

"Something that Mr. Dumpling told us," Sarah muttered under her breath. "He was drunk from eating overcooked marshmallows."

"Anyway," Selena interrupted loudly, a bit too loud for my taste. "What was I talking about again?"

"Oblivion being cruel," Yohan prompted.

"Oh, yeah. I don't really have much more to

say about that." We stayed silent for a few moments until I sparked up the conversation again by saying, "So are you really hurt right now. I mean, in poor medical condition?"

"That? No. I'm perfectly healed, but I still have memories. Terrible memories."

"You'll be fine. It's getting late, though. We better get to sleep." Sarah and Yohan nodded in agreement, wished us a good night, and headed back to the pathways.

"This was an interesting day," I said, sitting down on the rock next to her. "Well, it's just you and me again."

"Of course it is. These rocks are uncomfortable. How about let's find somewhere else to lay." We settled criss-cross applesauce in a lush patch of grass that overlooked the lake and gave us a clear view of the sky and stars.

"Why do you keep that cloak on? I mean, it makes you look cool, I mean, cooler than you were before- Whatever. Just ignore that, okay?" She smirked and nodded.

"I wear it as a reminder. In my opinion, it symbolizes who Oblivion really is. The outside is dark purple-" She held it up for me to me. "The inside is pure black. Just like how Oblivion is. He seemed like he would make the world a better place to his allies, but in his heart, he doesn't care, as long as he gets what he wants."

"That makes sense," I agreed. "We should be getting to sleep soon. Sarah's going to start yelling at us."

"Yes sir. I'm very tired- What happened to your shirt?" She stared at my back, which was now exposed because Oblivion had used my own weapon against me.

"Oblivion happened," I answered. "Do you mind if you summon in a new one for me, perhaps?"

"That will do." She raised her hand in the air, and a new, freshly washed white linen shirt magically appeared on my chest. My old Fort Azari shirt was gone from underneath.

"Thank you." I lay my back against a rock while Selena sat down next to me and put an arm around my shoulder.

We spent some time enjoying the vast expansive Milky Way that was glimmering above in the heavens. Selena edged closer and closer to me until we were right next to each other. It seemed that she didn't want to leave me after being gone for a few days, and to be honest, I didn't really want to leave her too. She buried her head in my shoulder and went to sleep.

I couldn't sleep. There were too many things buzzing around in my mind like fireflies.

Just relax, I told myself. *You're with your best friend right now. Enjoy the moment. Wait, what? I thought I just heard something.* Looking down, Selena was crying softly into my shirt.

"Hey," I whispered. "There's no need to hide your emotions from me. She looked up with twinkling black eyes just like the night sky.

Hold on, I thought. *Her eyes looked blue a few moments ago! How can that be?*

"Are you going to ask about my eyes?" she said. "I'll tell you why. After I... died, I went to the afterlife as a spirit. Then, when Signus shot me back to here, I lost some abilities and gained some abilities. Some things have changed. Now my eyes are the same color as the sky is, all the time. When I talked about Kam, that wasn't Oblivion influencing me. It's just me, now, and I was kind of afraid that you didn't like the new me."

"That's why? Don't worry, Selena. I'll always like you, however you change. Except when you were Oblivion."

"Oh, thanks. If you didn't notice, even my hair changed color, but it isn't so obvious."

"Wait. Did you lose your brand, too?" A year ago, in our efforts in retrieving Vesuvius, Yharon's defense mechanism had left a brand on each of our wrists, basically screaming "Monsters, come here! Fresh demigod meat, buy one get one free!"

"That's still here, but it used to be on my right wrist. Now it's on my left wrist. I hate this. Once I see the tiny Oblivion again, I will pummel him into the Endless Abyss so he'll be forever falling."

"Two things. First, how is Oblivion not destroyed yet? I thought-"

"He's a god," she explained. "No matter what you do, he won't just be gone. I'm pretty sure I saw somebody throw him into a bottle and take him away."

"Great. The next thing, we went to the bottom of the Endless Abyss when you were gone."

"Really? That's kind of an oxymoron."

"What's an oxymoron?"

"It's a figure of speech where two contradictory words appear- never mind. I'll give you a lesson on it when I teach you grammar and composition, so maybe you can write a book about my amazing adventures!"

"Maybe I will," I responded, as if sitting in a classroom listening to Selena babble about pronouns and gerunds was a reasonable idea. "Thinking about it, though, we do have to go back down there are untie Alumenta from her bonds." She made a sound that was almost as bad as my donkey-getting-hit-by-a-car impression when she hugged me after coming back up from the dead. "What?"

"You see..." I began retelling the long tale of us going to the monster-infested University of San Diego, facing off Elf Guy (a.k.a. Aggergard), destroying the building (that part was really important), heading over to Alumenta, blowing her palace to smithereens (that part was also important), free-falling into the Endless Abyss, and just overall having a poor time.

"You did all this without me?" she said. "I'm so proud of you, Will. I always thought you needed me to be your parent."

"Sarah's already enough. Another one will make my brain explode."

"Not that your brain much use anyway," she noted. "Sorry. But still, it's true. How about we sleep?"

"Sleep would be good."

"Alright then. It's decided. No talk. Sleep." She curled up on the grass next to me, and we both fell fast asleep.

. . .

Of course I appeared in Selena's dream. It was just my luck too, because her dream was even more horrific than ever before.

At first, it was just all dark around me, and it felt like I was falling endlessly. Then I realized, this was what Selena was feeling when she was possessed by Oblivion.

"What is this?" I murmured. Something brushed against my back. I turned. Selena was dropping downwards along with me, and her face was a blend of pure terror and fright.

"No. Not again. I can't have this again." I reached out and touched her lightly, but she flinched and swatted my hand away. "You're not Will. You're Oblivion. I remember you. You're here to cause misery."

"What? No. Don't you remember, Selena? It's me, Will, your friend. I'm here to help-"

"GO AWAY!" she screamed. Her words were like a sharp wind that blasted me back. "You're not Will, you're just trying to trick me!"

Suddenly, the darkness flickered and revealed a sight of me holding an elemental dagger, staring at us in the dream.

The image faded, and the void below us turned white and solid. Soon we were standing in a completely blank room, with a very hostile Selena glaring at me.

"Selena, please," I begged. "You have to understand. I'm not Oblivion, I'm just Will. This is just a dream-" She faltered for a moment when I said that, but her intimidating stare stayed strong as ever after that second.

"You are not Will. Even if you are Will, which you're not, why would you put me through this? Why would you make me suffer through all of Oblivion's horrors? You're just trying to play with my mind, Oblivion."

What? I thought. *Does she resent me now because I put her through all of her sufferings? No she wouldn't.*

"I HATE YOU!" she screamed, so resounding that the dream shook. "I HATE YOU, WILL!"

I didn't know if she meant it, but I didn't have any time to think about it because the white room faded and revealed the green field of grass that we were sleeping on. It was still dark, with the sunrise slowly creeping up over the mountain peaks.

Selena was gasping and choking like she had just swallowed a ghost pepper (Yohan tried once, and he started to blow fire)(that's also why one of our apartment walls is charred and black) and started sobbing into my chest.

"I'm- I'm sorry," she muttered into my shirt. "I- I didn't mean too. I'm sorry."

"It's okay," I whispered, though I wasn't really listening to her apology.

Does she hate me? Does she hate me for sending Oblivion's spirit into her body? She can't hate me.

"Will. I know what you're thinking, but I don't hate you. I don't resent you for doing what you did. Please! Listen to me!" I was staring up into the heavens, talking to myself, oblivious to what she was saying until she waved her hands in my face and shouted, "Earth to Will!"

"Huh?" I looked down at Selena's beautiful face, her eyes that were slowly turning to the orange and red hues of the sunrise but shimmering with tears, and knew that it would be impossible not to forgive her. She wasn't speaking the truth in the dream.

"Please, please forgive me. I mean, I didn't mean it. I thought- I thought this was some sort of trick. Oblivion played mind games with me like that before. He always sent the people dearest: my mom, my dad, you, sometimes Sarah and Yohan and Zach. I thought that you were one of the apparitions-" I didn't even ask what apparition meant. "-that he summoned to taunt me. And the fakes were always so pleading, just like how you acted- I- I- can't. I just... I don't know." She held her head as if it was going to explode.

Her emotions, her everything was so thrown out of whack and messed up that I didn't know what to say.

"I should be the one saying sorry. I was the one who put you through all of this, after all. But just to make you happy, I'm sorry. But I don't deserve to receive an apology from you."

"Thank- thank you." She put her head in my shirt and wrapped her arms around me. We just stayed like that for a long while, until Abaddon teleported in front of us, looking a bit (a bit is an understatement) cross in his purple cloak and two swords.

"There she is!" he roared. Selena looked up at the god. "The girl who escaped death."

"What are you doing here?" she snapped, getting up off the ground and giving Abaddon a death stare. I was a bit disappointed when she got up, because we were in a comfortable position there. "Aren't you supposed to be dealing with all the deaths along with Signus instead of talking with us puny demigods?"

"As for that, Signus has been severely punished for letting the dead come back, actually, he'll be a butterfly for a few weeks. And I have more important things to deal than deal with the deaths. Perhaps, take back the escaped dead." A cold hand clamped over my heart again. He couldn't just take Selena from me. He couldn't.

"NO!" I said defiantly, standing protectively in front of Selena. "After all we've been through, you are not taking her back." I remembered what had defeated Abaddon: anger. Could I defeat him again?

"I'm sorry, kid. Rules are rules." Anger and rage sucked up in my chest and exploded out.

In one moment, Abaddon had been blasted with a beam of elemental energy, disarmed of his two trusty blades, and pushed to the ground with dagger at his throat.

"Do you want to think again?" I snarled.

"Nobody takes my friends. Nobody."

"Okay," he gulped. "Never mind, then." He attempted to shove me off of him but was held tight.

"Don't you dare hurt her, or I'll get you again, understand? And next time, you won't be as lucky."

"I'm a god, kid-"

"Don't call me kid. And I don't care if you're god, gods are still arrogant. Oblivion was right about that, at least."

"Okay, okay. Now let me get back up."

"Say please."

"Please." I nodded and got back off the grass, brushing myself off. Selena smirked at me and said, "You've learned some things from me."

"No! This is all self-taught," I protested.

"Sure." She laughed.

"So." Abaddon cleared his throat. "You can talk about that stuff later on your own time. The problem that I was going to talk about was about Alumenta. She's still down in that cursed place, wanting to be freed, screaming about how she needs a new manicure after her nails got broken, that kind of stuff. Maybe she's a bit salty about her power loss."

"What do you mean, power loss?" I asked.

"She was one of the goddesses that gained power when Oblivion gained power. Unfortunately, Oblivion now doesn't have any power, so we've all received a loss of power."

"So that's why you're so stumpy right now," I mumbled.

"Excuse me?"

"Nothing," I said coolly, taking out my dagger and casually looking at it. "Continue on."

"Well, I need you to get down there and convince her that Oblivion is defeated and she should return to the right side!"

"Why don't you just do it," I challenged. "We're doing more important things." I didn't know what we were going to do today, but I really didn't want to venture back to that horrid place.

"My speaking skills aren't great," he admitted, obviously telling a fib. "Also, I have to go prepare for the New Year Festival at Aer's palace."

"And when is that?"

"The night of the thirtieth."

"That's stupid. Why wouldn't it be on the thirty-first, the actually New Year?" I probably should have been a bit more respectful, but I didn't feel like being considerate after completing such a difficult task.

"I don't know." He shrugged. "Not my plan. Well, I'm transferring you two down there now. Enjoy your visit!"

Chapter 15

Hint: If you want to enjoy a day out with your best friend, I would not recommend going to the bottom of the Endless Abyss.

"So... This is it. By the way, what's the date again?" She looked around at the bleak landscape of charred cinder trees and dark grass along with the millions of spirits aimlessly floating around.

"It's the twenty-ninth."

"What?" she gasped. "That's my birthday!"

Really? I scolded myself. *I don't even know my best friend's birthday? That's just terrible.*

"Oh, I... I didn't get a present for you," I mumbled. That was pretty obvious.

"Really? You just defeated the world's worst villain and you're worried about getting me a present? Don't worry. You being with me is the best gift."

"Thanks." I blushed. "I- Thanks."

"So what are we looking for down here, again?"

"Maybe..." In the dark horizon, a swirling hurricane of all types of runes was clumping together in a colorful monstrosity above the ruins of Alumenta's castle. "How about we go there?"

Yep, I regret heading down to this atrocious place for Selena's birthday. Going to some restaurant and relaxing with some pizza and my friends were more of my style.

At least hanging out in the Endless Abyss gave us a very long time to talk, so I decided to strike up a conversation.

"Zach said that there was a disease eating at your heart. What did he mean?" She was silent for a moment, and it seemed that the only sound anywhere was coming from the crunch of black pebbles under our feet.

"Okay. I'll admit it. So, when David- when David was free of Oblivion, Zach detected this sickness in his body.

"And how do you know this, again? You were possessed by Oblivion."

"I had a dream about it. But that's not important. The disease was eating away at his soul, his essence. That's what made him… die."

"Wait. You you have the same disease?"

"Unfortunately, yes I do. But we don't know how bad it's affecting me right now, because, well-" She spread out her arms. "I'm not dead, as you can see."

"So…"

"I don't know. Zach knows of a Grovite living in China that might be able to help me, but that's for another day. For now, let's focus- whoa!" She nearly stepped into a gaping crevice in the middle of the earth. Far down below, magma bubbled and popped like an inviting cauldron of stew.

"Let's not do that," I said, pulling her back. "It appears that we have arrived. And this whole place is surrounded by a ravine. How fabulous."

"Runes. We'll get across this with runes. Stand back." She cast a different rune that I had never seen before and created a blue holographic bridge across the chasm.

"Is that safe?" I wondered.

"No time! We have to get going!" she urged. Sure enough, the railings were fading and turning into runes that were sucked into the swirling vortex ahead. We dashed across right as the bridge crumbled.

"Manicure!" Alumenta screamed from somewhere inside the ruins over the piercing winds flinging runes everywhere. "My nails are ruined! I demand justice! Ahhhh…" It sounded as if she was trying to sing alto with no pitch whatsoever.

"That sounds like her," Selena mumbled. "But last time she was so calm, so serene-" A destroy rune exploded in our faces and turned a brick into charred cinders.

"How about we hide, first. Or we end up like that brick down there." We ducked into an unharmed passage and sat for a little talk.

"Alumenta- She isn't like this. Something's affecting her."

"Gee, I wonder," I said. "Maybe it's the fact that she's stuck in this pit of eternal death and can't get out. Or maybe because she lost most of her power and is now mad at us."

"Yeah, I wonder too. How about we check her out without getting impaled by any of these runes?"

"Good idea. Let's go now." We slowly forged our way toward the eye of the storm: a tiny ring where the raging storm didn't rain runes upon the ground. Alumenta was bound there, somehow standing up even with her chains, screeching about needing a new manicure.

"Alumenta!" I called.

"Hmm?" She turned to us, and the storm momentarily stopped, releasing a shower of runes onto the ground. "Aha! It's you two, the two who bound me! I will break free soon and get a new manicure from Sir Dumpling the Great!" She launched a high-velocity rune at me, and I just stared, paralyzed.

As quick as lightning, Selena flung out her cloak and deflected the blast into a wall.

"So your cloak is bullet-proof," I noted. "Nice to know."

"Yeah! Great! Now what do we do? And Mr. Dumpling is a marshmallow melting maniac, why would you want to talk to him?"

"He is a very respected gentleman, and his

cooking will give you superpowers!" I wished I knew that when I faced that cavern of angry ice wolves.

"AHA!" Alumenta screeched. The bonds fell off her wrists and ankles. "I am free! I will go awaken the Runists and create the Runic Maelstrom once again!"

"What?" Selena paled as if she had said, "I will destroy the universe!" or something like that.

"Um... what does maelstrom mean? And-" She shot me a look that told me to shut my mouth up.

"So long, suckers!" She flew into the air with the swirling storm still roaring above her and floated away.

"This... this is bad." I definitely could tell, as her face was extremely pale and full of fear.

"So, what is this Runic Maelstrom thing? And again, what does maelstrom mean?"

"A maelstrom is a storm or whirlpool in the sea. Now, the Runic Maelstrom is something even worse. So, there's this group of magicians called the Runists. They studied runes and used to be on the god's side. Then they had different ideas. They used their runic power to create a storm so powerful that no god or goddess could beat. And that was how Alumenta was born. She stopped the storm, sent the Runists into exile, and built her kingdom."

"So another huge task to do?"

"We'll save that for another day," she answered, as if it was a homework assignment due next week. "For now, let's enjoy my birthday. Perhaps there's a tourist shop here where we can get magazines that tell us the best places to tour."

...

Unfortunately for us, there was a tourist shop nestled next to large, sloshing, winding river of gurgling lava and a grove of severely abnormal deformed pale trees with absolutely no leaves on them. Well again, what did I expect?

The visitor center wasn't any more pretty, with black stone walls like basalt or that wall in my home that Yohan had set on fire and a low, red roof made out of shingles.

Once we walked up the gravel path to the building, Selena tried the tinted glass doors that led inside and shook her head. "It's closed. Let's break in."

"Wait, what?" I protested. "You can't just do that!"

"After destroying that other visitor center, you think I care much about this place?" She laughed. "Will, please use your brain." With the snap of her finger, the glass shattered.

"How'd you do that?"

"Oh, it's all about modifying the air pressure

and… I'm sure you don't want to hear about it, but I just can do it."

"Let's go." As soon as we stepped inside the building, lights flared on and revealed a front desk table along with a shop loaded with souvenirs. A case sat on the left of us holding a variety of rocks, bones, and other nerdy stuff. And of course, there were the brochures.

"Here we go," Selena said happily, snatching one of the pamphlets. "So, let's see."

"Nerd," I muttered under my breath.

"Mount You Are Going To Die," Selena read. "Erupts every other second. Pyroclastic flow temperatures reaching twenty-thousand degrees."

"Very ominous," I noted. "By the way, what's pyroclastic flow?"

"Haven't you been listening in Earth science at school?" she scolded. "Pyroclastic flow is fast moving debris and volcanic ash that travels down a volcano at high speeds. Highly dangerous."

"That's awesome. What else is there to tour?"

"So, we got the bottom of the bottom of the Endless Abyss, five miles away, and the bottom of the bottom of the bottom of the Endless Abyss. We're standing right on top of it, except it's a few hundred miles down. You want to go there?"

"I'd rather not," I responded.

"Here's a photograph of it." She showed me

a laminated card that was just completely pitch black. "And- oh! There's a place here where all the Runists were chained. It's in Aurora Valley, apparently, which is only a mile's worth of walking from here. Let's go." She took my hand, and we began the long trek to the valley.

Of course, my mind drifted off to other thoughts. This time, it was about school.

Since Selena's rented apartment near our apartment was being used again, they had to move into our place. Of course, Selena's dad thought that it was a huge hassle to my mom for staying there (though I must admit that I enjoyed Selena's company) and wanted to get back to New York as soon as possible. They had already shipped most their furniture to New York and were going to leave right after Christmas. Then this little problem popped up, and here we were.

But in school, the girls and boys were all divided against each other. The girls thought the boys had cooties, the boys thought that the girls were stupid, and so on. That wasn't the case for Selena and me. We were best friends and always talked to each other at lunch, helped each other in schoolwork, greeted each other in the hallway. Because of the division between the boys and girls, we were treated like outcasts, different than the rest of the crowd.

Would we ever be treated like normal people,

even if we're not? I thought. *Of course in Fort Azari, people would think that you're normal, but in the outside world...* I hated being left out by other people.

"We have arrived," Selena announced. As I looked up, my grasp tightened on Selena's hand.

In front of us, the void had parted, revealing a night sky rippled with green and yellow lights. Down below was a peaceful valley with a river running through its center and a quaint village along the side. Vast trees shot out of the ground, some even bigger than the big tree at Sequoia. Birds chirped. I thought I even saw a fox running and giving some berries to a rabbit.

"We could live here," she whispered. "We could stay here, and all our problems would be over."

"Hey, snap out of it," I said. "We're not here to live here. We just need to find the Runist's headquarters whatcha-ma-call-it."

"Huh? Oh. Okay. Sorry."

As we entered into the forest landscape, the air rippled behind us. I turned and tried to walk back out but bumped into an invisible wall.

"Well, it looks like we're stuck here for a while."

We slowly tramped down the path to the meander of a river which then led to the tiny village. I couldn't believe that the people who tried to destroy the world now lived in such a serene place like this. I was imagining more of a haunted house feel.

"So when did the Runists do their thing?" I asked.

"A long while ago, in the eleven hundreds. You know about the Black Death?" I didn't know about the Black Death. "That was caused by them."

"And what's the Black Death?"

"It's complicated, but a bunch of people died. A third of Europe's population was wiped out. Even now, there are some smaller versions of the Runic Maelstrom. Hurricanes. Earthquakes."

"But aren't earthquakes and stuff caused by plates in the ground?"

"You aren't completely clueless," she said. "But that scientific stuff is just a cover-up story. And- Oh man, what the heck are they doing?" A group of people, clothed in colorful robes with runes fluttering around them were chanting around a stone altar.

"Whoa," I whispered. "What in the world are they doing?"

"This is not good."

"Alumenta!" one of the Runists bellowed. "We have called for you for one thousand years! Even though you have cast us into a shameful exile,we still believe in you as the most powerful goddess! Answer us!"

There was silence for a moment, and a voice spoke. "I will come. Together, we will crush the Earth."

More silence. Then, wild cheering erupted from the crowd.

"We knew you were going to answer one day!" the person cried. "Thank you, thank you!"

The altar exploded into more runes which immediately drifted away as if it was being pulled by a magnetic forcefield. Suddenly, all the runes floating around everyone started flying away. The Runists gazed in awe as the night sky was blotted by great rainbow storm clouds and a figure in colorful robes.

"I am here!" Alumenta declared. "I have gotten my manicure from Sir Dumpling and will now lead us to victory!"

"Who are you two?" a gruff, deep voice growled. "Newcomers?"

We turned and came face to face with the guy who did all the chanting earlier. Up close, he had a rust-colored long beard and a timeless face,even though he looked pretty old. My only response was, "Uh…"

"Were you spirits who entered into this place, thinking it would lead you back to the overworld? Yes, you would be reborn into flesh and skin, but you would be trapped here."

"What?" Nothing he said made any sense.

"You see, Alumenta created this place here so that we could live here forever. If we stay here, we are immortal, never dying. But if any spirits enter here, they join the Runists. So who are you?"

"Um… I'm Will. This is my sister-" I winced when I said that. "Selena."

"Really? Interesting. Stay out of harm's way, because Alumenta is coming down." We took that as an invitation to run into the forest and hide.

After taking refuge on the highest hill under the tallest oak in the grove, I finally took a deep breath.

"I'm your sister now?" she said. "When did you get that idea?" I could tell that she was trying not to burst out laughing.

"Sorry. My mind was a bit frazzled there."

"That's great. Now serious talk. What do we do?"

"I always thought you were the one with the plans," I complained.

"Well, Alumenta's going to come in, free all of these Runists, and conquer the world. We can't stop her from doing that. I mean, we can stop her from destroying the world, but we can't do anything else. Let's just focus on doing this stuff."

"Yeah," I mumbled. "Sure."

"Hey, what's wrong?"

"Just sorry for dragging you along on this crazy journey for your birthday. You should just be at Fort Azari or some restaurant singing and enjoying time with your friends, not this!"

"Are you not my friend? Don't worry, Will, this is my best birthday ever."

"Thanks." I blushed. "So-" The tree got ripped from its anchor to the ground and was sucked into Alumenta's storm.

"Come to me, demigod cowards!" Alumenta roared. She was spinning in the air, her cloak flashing in a million different directions while the Runists floated alongside her. "Fight me!" She pointed a finger and sent a blast of red lightning into Selena's chest, sending her tumbling down the hill.

"Hey!" I shouted. "You come to us! I can't even reach you!" Yeah, I know, I sounded like a complaining baby.

"Nah, I'd rather not," she cackled, sending another bolt of magic at my face. I countered back with a powerful burst of elemental energy that exploded in her face.

"Gah!" she yelped. "Not fair! Run away!" She flew away in her massive maelstrom, carrying the Runists along with her.

"What was that?" Selena groaned. She was back up the hill with grass and leaves stuck in her hair and a very charred shirt. "Did Alumenta just-"

"Yeah, she did. Now we have to save the world again."

"Again, that's for another day. How about

some birthday cake in this awesome valley? By the way, we also have to find the way out of here. I mean, Alumenta did just take the Runists with her, but we're still here." With a swipe of her hand, a whole meal of some bread, cheese, fresh fruit, and a nice, little vanilla cake appeared along with some lemonade.

"How can you-"

"It's my mom's blessing. She's- Oh! I have to see her. She has to be back to normal, right?"

"Yeah... She should be." I knew I should have been excited that Aer was back, but I was afraid after being mortal enemies with her.

"Whatever. How about we eat?" The food tasted heavenly, but I had been living on energy bars and chocolate for the past few days so my taste buds probably thought that burnt peanuts tasted good.

After that, we split the cake in half and ate it slowly. It was like a fluffy sponge cake, tasting absolutely amazing. I was going to need to ask Aer for her recipe.

As soon as Selena touched hers, it turned into a pile of gray ash. She yelped and brushed it aside.

"I have no idea how I did that. Either, mind if you share some of your slice?" I nodded and gave her a crumb.

"Bigger than that."

I gave her another crumb.

"Bigger." I split my slice in half and offered it to her (look how nice I am). We headed out of the hill with we on and explored the deep woods, admiring the beauty of nature. It reminded me a few days ago when we had walked down that path to the enemy base together at Sequoia. The scenes were both so peaceful, so tranquil that I wondered what else I was missing in life.

"Well," I gasped after tripping over the tenth root of a tree. "I think that's enough, dear sister. How about we see the Mount You Are Going To Die instead? Maybe it'll have paved paths."

Unfortunately, it did not have paved paths.

So, leaving Aurora Valley with actually a breeze. All the magical barriers were just gone, so we left with no problem. Isn't that just great? And then we moved on to that volcano that blew pyroclastic flow something-or-another. Turns out, it was black and charred to a crisp like one of Mr. Dumpling's marshmallows and was spewing green liquid. I was pretty sure the mystery substance wasn't green apple juice.

"How about we leave now?" I choked as dust filled up my lungs. "This is not good either."

"That will do." Abaddon appeared in front of us and winced. "Have you enjoyed your visit? I hope you have. Leave a five-star rating on Yharon Resorts, okay? It would really help our business. So where's Alumenta?"

"Good question," I snapped. "Maybe, if we had a god on our side to help instead of doing something else useless, Alumenta wouldn't be running around the world like a maniac along with her maniac Runists summoning the Runic Maelstrom and destroying the world."

"Oh, really? That's what happened? How inconsiderate of you."

"Oh, for Reality's sake, would you please shut up?" For once, Selena's shouting skills came in real handy. "It's not like you did any work! If you expected something good, just do it yourself, idiot!"

"I wouldn't say that," Abaddon warned, but he sounded frightened. "I did come here to take you to that New Years party. It's the thirtieth, you know."

"What? How did that much time pass?"

He shrugged. "Time is weird here in the Endless Abyss, just like Alluvion's department store. Sometimes it goes super slow, sometimes, it just whizzes past. You know, once I came down here. It was about the year one thousand, I think. Then I went for a vacation down in the Burning Hotel, and when I had slept for a night a century had passed. I missed the Crusades, man! It sucked."

"So you left us down here," Selena said. "Knowing that we might live through a century without realizing it? Really?" She looked just about ready to slap him in his shadowy face.

"I'm sorry, honey, but you'll just have to deal with it."

"Don't call me honey!"

"Okay honey. Well, I'm here to bring you up to the New Year celebration at Aer's palace. By the way, the new palace looks sick. It's- Actually, you should just see for yourself."

"My mom!" Selena gasped. "I have to see her! I know I said that like ten times in the past hour, but-"

"You said it once," I noted.

"Yeah? So? I don't-"

"Just forget it."

"Then let's go!" Abaddon said. With a wave of his hand, we were transported back to Aer's palace.

Chapter 16

Now, this place was amazing. Incredible. Stunning. Extraordinary. (I'm running out of words to describe it.)

A circular white marble all surrounded the whole place, sort of like those old Roman amphitheaters, except one hundred times cooler. In the center sat a four-story tall white open-air pagoda looking structure, completely different than Aer's old castle but completely better. Surrounding it was a large courtyard covered with food of all sorts: sushi (my favorite), pasta (my second favorite), eggs (my least favorite), and other things. Hanging above the courtyard were orange lanterns swaying in the breeze and casting a warm ambiance upon the island. A band played some violin music in the background while some danced slowly to the tune. In the distance were gardens filled with fresh, blooming flowers kept in with little fences.

At the bottom floor of the pagoda, the thrones of the gods and goddesses all sat facing the honorary seat for Earth. Most of the demigods had arrived already and were eating, chatting, or turning each other into rats (that was a new one to me).

"Mom!" Selena cried. She rushed at a regal lady wearing a white gown who was serving herself some water.

"Who-" She turned and broke into a smile. "Selena! Oh, honey, thank goodness!" I decided to go and find my own dad, Galaxius. He was standing next to Cryos wearing a formal black suit with a white collared shirt underneath.

"Dad!" I called.

"Will?" He strode toward me and patted my back. "You did a good job. You managed to do what none of us even could do, and I'm proud of you for that."

"It's the demigod show-off again, huh?" Cryos hissed. "This time, we'll turn you into a delicious-"

"Please give him a break," my dad sighed. "Just let him be." That was it. No, "Get away from my kid!" No punching Cryos in her godly face. Oh well.

I went off to help myself to unlimited sushi, which was much better than the granola bars but just somehow not as nice as Selena's summoned meal at the Aurora Valley.

"Hey." Selena tapped on my shoulder. "Do you want to… you know. Dance?"

"What? I-"

"Don't look so surprised, Mumbo Jumbo."

"But I don't know how," I complained.

"You'll be fine," she assured. "I'll guide you." She took my hand, and we began slow-dancing to the music.

It must have been a weird sight: two teens, one wearing a dark cape, dancing under orange light on a floating island.

"One thing you never told me was why you paled when Rowen said Kam's name," I said.

"Don't you remember? Paul talked about his little sister, Kam. And here's Kam. They're both related to Alluvion. It all fits."

"Oh- Oh my. That's- Wow, I'm stupid. I can't believe I didn't realize that. Do we tell them?"

"We'll let them figure out themselves, Will. And see, you're dancing fine. But you keep stepping on my feet."

"Sorry, sorry." I grinned at her. Then some demigod or god called out, "Everyone, come to the palace!"

"I enjoyed dancing with you," she said. "Maybe we can try another time, and you won't step on my feet." She still held my hand, and we headed to the palace.

Seated in a semicircle were Reality and Galaxius in the middle, Aphelion, Abaddon, Alluvion, and Abyssion to the left and Aquaia, Aer, and Cryos to the right. Signus was nowhere to be seen, all though I was pretty sure I saw a giant monarch butterfly fluttering around earlier. I hoped that none of the demigods had taken it home for a pet.

"We have come," Reality announced in his green suit and pants and fabric. "To celebrate the victory over evil, all thanks to our fellow demigods."

All the gods and goddesses cheered in agreement except for Cryos who said something about demigods having stinky feet and smelling like carrots.

Reality then began rattling a long speech about how brave Abyssion and Aquaia were for defending the world's vast oceans, how valiant Aphelion fought against all the odds, how useful Abaddon was to aid in all of the skirmishes happening, how utterly useless Signus was while he was enjoying Las Vegas ("He wasted a million dollars just to earn a million dollars. How's that?"), how Aer stayed firm against the fierce attacks of Oblivion, how Cryos managed to fell thousands of monsters with only her scepter and with no help whatsoever from two demigods called Will Hanson and Selena Mayne, and finally how the demigods acted bravely in the circumstances. The part about the demigods was about one percent of the speech.

"And we would like to thank some people for their help specially. Selena Mayne, would you please come forward?" She let go of my hand and slowly knelt before the gods.

"Aha!" Cryos shrieked. "She bears the symbols of Oblivion! See her cape? Traitor!" She was immediately bound like a silvery linen mummy, courtesy of Alluvion.

"Please shut up, dear Cryos."

"Mmm-mmm!"

"Selena," Aer said. "You have been tortured and marred for life by Oblivion when you received his soul. In fact, you have been killed by him and risen again by Signus." A butterfly flew next to Aer and seemed to bow.

"We want to ensure with you that you will not be brought back from the living," Reality boomed while glaring at Abaddon. "You have done the gods great deeds. Thank you."

She returned back to her place and smiled at me. At least she wouldn't be leaving me for a while.

"Next up, Yohan Westwood!" Aphelion beckoned for him to come up. "After the death of our last head of the Aphelists, we needed a new one. Now, you-" He began a long list of formalities. "-are officially the head of all the Aphelists."

"Sarah Miller!" Reality called. "You are to be the second-in-command under Yohan because he is slightly disorganized and needs help keeping his head on his neck, as some have told." Nina and her group of friends snickered. I was pretty sure that Yohan and Sarah wanted to drop them into a nice pot of bubbling magma.

"Will Hanson!" Galaxius said.

"I guess they saved the best for last," Selena

whispered.

"Second best," I corrected. "You're the best." (Oh yes, I did just say that.) I went up in front of the gods and bowed before them.

"Will, my son. You have managed to stop an impending disaster. For that, we give you our deepest thanks. The gift we have for you… well… We grant you any gift that is within our power."

"Then could you bring back the dead? Like Hannah-" Abaddon and the butterfly shook their heads no. My heart sank.

"The dead must stay dead, unfortunately," Abaddon snapped. "We are not bringing back any more people."

"Um… Then can you ensure that all the people vacationing and living in the places that we've been will be safe? We caused quite a mess."

"That we can do. Thank you. You made a wise decision, Will." I left the presence of the gods and went back to my seat.

"Thank you for coming! Meeting adjourned!"

"That was a wise choice, Will," Selena praised. "Maybe you're growing."

"Of course I am!"

We spent the rest of the night strolling through the endless gardens and looking at the beautiful flowers blooming. Once, when Selena touched a rose, it crumbled into black ash.

"Whoa." She grabbed my arm.

"Please don't turn me into black dust too. Or my shirt. That would be embarrassing."

"I'll try." Snow began falling upon the island, blanketing it in a thin layer of frost. "We're entering the Alaska area right now. You know, this thing about turning objects into dust. It worries me. I have it under control currently, but if it gets too crazy, then…" I could tell what she meant.

"So, is the turning things to dust power related to your sickness? Well, of course it is. But it seems more of a bonus than a bad thing to your body. It's kind of like that Midas guy, could turn things into gold by touching them."

"That's an interesting way to describe it, but yes, it's sort of true. At least it doesn't happen all the time."

"Then how will you fix it?" I asked.

"That Grovite in China. He's a healer, so hopefully he'll know what's wrong."

"Awesome. It's getting late. How about we head back to Fort Azari and sleep?"

…

So, yeah. We defeated Oblivion. The world wasn't destroyed.

After an awesome New Years Eve at Fort Azari, my mom requested for me to head back home for the rest of winter. Randy agreed without hesitation, and I was back at Los Angeles by the first of January.

"Where is he? Where is he?" My mom rushed out of the apartment building and wrapped me in a hug. "My baby!"

"Thanks, thanks, mom." I was glad to see her too. "How about we talk inside?"

She made me retell my whole story from the beginning to the end. I teared up a bit at some parts but got through the entirety of it in one piece.

"I was so worried," she said. "The television kept on replaying the tsunami at Oceanside, and the weird image of two people flying straight into it."

"That was me."

"At the end they said it was a mirage. Mortals. It's always hilarious seeing how oblivious they are to the real world."

"Yeah." When I looked at her joyous face, I was ashamed of myself to ruin her good mood.

"Will, what's wrong?"

"It's Selena. She has this disease after being possessed by Oblivion, and I'm not sure how bad it is."

"That's so sweet of you, caring for her. I'm sure she'll be fine," she assured. "She's a strong girl."

"But mom, she can turn things into dust with her fingers? Isn't that just… scary?"

Instead of answering, she just sighed and

said, "I'm sorry for putting you through all this. You shouldn't have experienced this as a child."

"Mom, I'm not a child anymore. I'm thirteen!"

"But you're still my baby." (Well, this is getting embarrassing.) "We need to get dressed, honey. We're having dinner with Mr. Mayne tonight. They're leaving for New York tomorrow."

"For real now? Gosh, I'll miss her."

"We need to hurry. It's a six o'clock, and I booked a seat at this fancy restaurant! We need to do your hair, get you dressed up…" Man, my mother is great, but she's just too motherly sometimes. Sorry mom!

Selena left for New York the next day, but she promised to visit me whenever she had a chance with Darkecho's new nest on top of the Empire State Building. A part of me wanted to question how that worked, but I decided not to.

A few weeks later, on the afternoon of January twenty-third, I got a pleasant surprise. The doorbell rang, and I scurried over to answer it. I opened the door to find Selena smiling at me, wearing her regular Fort Azari white shirt and jeans along with her cloak. My heart did a happy flop when I saw her because I dearly missed her. (I know, it had only been a few weeks, but still.)

"Hey," she said. "Nice seeing you again." She held out her hands for a quick hug, and I embraced her. I immediately began trying to brush down my messy hair, but she just shook her head. "Will, please. I've been with you long enough to see one million of your bad hair days. Don't worry."

"Yeah! Sure! Uh... hi." Well, this conversation was turning out great.

"Can you come with me for few hours? We're going to take a quick stop at Fort Azari. Then there's this awesome place I want to show you."

"Mom!" I called. "I'm going out with Selena, okay?"

"Okay! Come back at six, honey! I'm going to cook a nice dinner for you! Also, Selena, you can stay for dinner if you want!" You might think, that's not a responsible mom, letting her kid run off with her friend. But she knew me. I often had to go off on random side quests, so this wasn't much of a worry.

"Thanks for the offer, Mrs. Hanson," she responded. "I'll be sure to stay for a bit."

"Thanks, mom! I love you!" We rushed out of the building, and Selena led me to a beige colored Toyota Highlander.

"Where in the world do you get that car?" I demanded. "I mean, it's cool. Also, who's going to drive?"

"Wait and see." She opened the backseat, let both of us in, and peered over the driver's seat.

"Remember Nimbus, the dog from Cryos?"

"Uh… yes."

"Well, he is technically sixteen in dog years, so he's going to drive." But then I nearly had a heart attack but kept my cool.

"Excuse me? That's- That's- well… That's expected from you." Nimbus sat on his haunches, sniffed my hands, and started to bite them. I guessed that that pork rib from yesterday really tasted good.

"He's a cute little thing," Selena said. "Adorable." Nimbus growled, apparently telling us that he wasn't a cute little thing and that he was a ferocious wolf ready to bring down his prey.

"And where'd you get the car?"

"A San Diegan genius friend let me have it. She's amazing at science, math, everything. She rented me this car- Well, her mom did. So we drove over here in a few minutes, and-"

"How do you drive one hundred miles in a few minutes?" I interrupted. "That's not possible."

"Well, with a bit of tweaking with the crankshaft and some magic-"

"Please no rocket science."

"It's not rocket science," she protested. "It's… uh… car science. Totally different stuff."

"And your genius friend trusted you that a puppy could drive a car? Not very genius."

She shrugged. "She knows I'm different. A

very brilliant mortal."

"Sure. How about we get on with this ride and get to that awesome place you were talking about."

"Okay. Nimbus, we're ready to go!" I'm not sure how an ice poodle could reach the wheel without wearing high heels, but he somehow managed it. As we veered precariously around traffic and didn't stop at stop signs (I think Nimbus only broke the traffic laws about one hundred times), I decided to spend some quality time talking with my best friend.

"So, how's school? Your new school."

"School? Oh, it's fine. There are some people there who I want to blast to bits, but I'm not going to." I peered out the window and watched the rolling grass hills fly by with the Sierra Nevadas in the background while violently bumping up and down thanks to the puppy's driving skills.

"So, why are we coming to Fort Azari first?" I asked as it came into view. The stone battlements of the walls seemed to have expanded all the way past the Aphelist's mountain and to the distant peaks. In fact, the walls had expanded a long bit.

"As you can see, the demigods have been hard at work. They've added a long wall expansion, along with an Alluvion cabin and keep in the mountains. The cabin is also going to serve as a place where we can retreat to in case… well… you

280

know what."

"Woof!" Nimbus barked, signaling that we had arrived. He ran over a couple logs lying on the ground for good measure, parked the car halfway on a boulder, and instantly started snoring away in his seat.

"Such a cutie," Selena said. "Sorry. Let's get going." We passed through the iron gates to a new dirt path that led to each of the demigod cabins. All the grass was well trimmed, the bushes all orderly. In other words, it was amazing.

"Geez," I mumbled. "They have done some work in a few weeks. This is insane."

"Yep," she agreed. "Let's bring you up to the mountain." As we walked up towards the Aphelist's base, I waved at my demigod friends and found a lot of new arrivals.

At the peak of the volcano, a rickety wooden path led to a one-story gray castle looking structure. Two walls with battlements stretched out and made a loop around a lower courtyard. From the peak, I could see all around the expanded Fort Azari, from Nina's ice cabin to the Aerialite cloud in the sky.

"We have to cross that?" I said. "No way."

Selena just rolled her eyes and pulled my hand to the bridge. "Please Will."

"Why is it designed like this?" I demanded.

"This is a place where we go for last resort. We all run across the bridge and cut the ropes.

Then, we'll have high ground over the rest of the enemy, and they won't be able to get here. Now let's go." She yanked me the whole way across, through the open door, and into a large living room type area. The floor was made out of wood, and a plush white carpet spanned most of the floor. On it sat a handful of white couches and chairs, with a flat-screen television playing the strange sighting of the two people flying into the Oceanside tsunami.

"We will be back with Steve for new weather reports," the woman on the television said. "Also, a brilliant science genius living in San Diego has discovered a secret with a type of pine tree…" The volume turned down.

There were multiple exits to the room, two doors leading out to the outer walls of the keep and a flight of stairs leading to the roof and down to the Alluvion living quarters.

"Cool place," I said. "So what's outside?" Outside was also just as grand as the inside. The courtyard set inside the wall had a fountain spraying mist in the air and another room filled with rows and rows of swords, spears, and armor.

"We're relocating the Meeting House to over here, just in case an attack happens."

"You seem really worried about attacks happening."

"The Runists are out, Will. The Runists are evil. They have evil minds. They might have seemed friendly, but they seek to destroy. Back then, Alumenta was a wise goddess. She didn't imprison the Runists for nothing. Now she's on their side, making them even more powerful. But they have a weakness to the air. Aer also wants to bring them back to imprisonment, so she's basically blocking off any form of air travel."

"That's why we have out base up here," I inferred. "So we'll have a bigger advantage."

"You're right for once. Anyways, this is Fort Azari now. Let's get to where we need to be before the sun sets."

"Sure. Back to Nimbus, I guess."

Once we were situated in the vehicle again, we had to wake Nimbus from his eternal slumber (which he was not happy about) and then have him start up the car again.

When we were cruising down a highway, purple mist swirled in the air and blotted out the windows. Weird sounds filled the air, and ghostly faces appeared at the windows.

"Uh… what is this?" The car started shaking and rattling like it was falling apart.

"The magic that we put in the car's engine," she replied. "As you can see, this is what it does. So we mixed some hydrochloric acid with some magical materials and put it in-"

"Sorry, Airhead," I said. "But I'm not interested. Very sorry." Nimbus started growling at a random leaf that blew onto the windshield. The smoke and fog cleared, revealing a paved road with the ocean and a beach on the left and hotels of all sorts on the right.

"Here we are," she announced. "San Diego. La Jolla, to be exact. I discovered this place a few months ago, and I would always have Nimbus drive me down. The view is amazing." As Nimbus attempted to park in a resident's driveway (if you see a home with a front yard covered in crushed flowers and plants, that's where we were), I just had to admire the golden sky streaked with crimson and magenta and filled with fluffy clouds.

"Woof!" Nimbus immediately fell asleep again. I opened the door and stepped out into the fresh ocean air.

"The thing is," Selena continued. "I always would come down here alone. I needed a friend with me just so I could enjoy the ocean with someone."

"Enjoy the ocean? But I thought you hated water."

"Well, this is the one place where Aquaia and I can live in harmony without bashing each other to pieces." She took my hand and led me down to a field where we sat on the lush grass.

"Without a doubt, I've missed a lot of things in the world," I said. "This is most definitely one of the places. The other was at Sequoia, when we went to the enemy base. Remember that?"

She nodded. "It seems so long ago now. That's crazy. It was only a month away."

"Oh well. For now, how about we enjoy this amazing view without people trying to destroy the world?"

"Oh yes, I will enjoy it."

She smiled at me with her eyes that were now flaming orange and pink. Everything had changed about her. Her hair color, her traits, everything.

Stop thinking that way, I scolded myself. *You just have to enjoy your life, because you never know what's coming up next.*

Those words of wisdom were absolutely correct. When you're a demigod, you never know what monster might be waiting for you, lurking in the shadows.

…

Well, there you have it, folks. That's why the world nearly ended in several different places, and that's also why you saw two people fly into a tsunami on the evening news.

If you think you're a demigod, try to find the Grovite at your school. He or she will help you to get safely to Fort Azari. We get new recruits every day, and we're always open for more. Come to Fort Azari. We'll be waiting for you.

99312107R00163

Made in the USA
Columbia, SC
07 July 2018